FINN PARKER
and the
Mystery in the Heart of Ravenrode

"In a town where secrets are buried, an ancient force is about to awaken."

Yaythish Kannaa G S

–※ CONTENTS ※–

–✳ CONTENTS ✳–

-※ CONTENTS ※-

THE HEART OF
RAVENRODE
THE HEART OF
LSOST GROVE
RAVEN
ITITIING GROVE
TRAINING GROV

RODE
TRAININ
GROVE
LOST GROVE

Prologue: The Celestial Event

On a clear night in the enchanting village of Ravenrode, the air crackled with a sense of magic and anticipation. It was a night unlike any other, marked by the rare celestial alignment of planets and stars, a phenomenon that occurred once in a generation. As the sun dipped below the horizon, the villagers gathered outside, their faces illuminated by the shimmering lights overhead.

Children danced in the streets, their laughter mingling with the whispers of the wind. Ravenrode was alive with excitement, its inhabitants aware that this was a night of significance. The elders had spoken of the legends surrounding the celestial event how children born under its glow would possess extraordinary gifts and a connection to one another that would last a lifetime.

As the night deepened, the sky transformed into a tapestry of vibrant colors. Streaks of brilliant blues, purples, and golds swirled together, casting an ethereal glow over the village. The stars twinkled like diamonds, illuminating the faces of the villagers, who gazed upward in awe.

In the heart of Ravenrode, candles flickered in windows, their warm light spilling into the streets, creating a soft, inviting atmosphere. The scent of blooming flowers and freshly baked bread filled the air, wrapping the village in a comforting embrace. Families gathered together, sharing stories and laughter, while the night sky performed its celestial dance.

As the clock struck midnight, a hush fell over the crowd. The villagers held their breath, eyes wide with wonder, as a brilliant flash of light erupted in the sky, cascading down like shooting stars. It illuminated the landscape, casting long shadows and igniting a spark of hope in every heart.

In that moment, five babies were born in different corners of Ravenrode, each heralded by the unique magic of the celestial event. Unbeknownst to the villagers, these five children would grow to share a profound bond, their destinies forever intertwined by the forces of magic and friendship.

As the night unfolded, the first cries of the newborns echoed softly through the village, each sound a promise of adventure and discovery. The villagers felt an unexplainable connection to these children, sensing that they were destined for greatness. With the stars twinkling above them, the village of Ravenrode stood on the brink of a new chapter, one that would be filled with wonder, mystery, and the unbreakable bonds of friendship.

Chapter 1

Sophie and the Enchanted Glade

As dawn broke over Ravenrode, a gentle rain began to fall, pattering softly against the rooftops and awakening the vibrant flowers that adorned the village. Inside a cozy cottage nestled at the edge of the enchanted forest, Sophie Bennett took her first breath, heralded by the soft glow of morning light filtering through the window.

The air was filled with the sweet scent of earth and blooming petals, creating an atmosphere that seemed to celebrate her arrival. As the midwife, a kind and elderly woman named Granny Hazel, cradled the newborn in her arms, she couldn't help but smile. "Ah, a flower child!" she exclaimed, sensing the magic that surrounded Sophie.

Sophie's parents, Lydia and Thomas Bennett, were filled with joy as they gazed upon their daughter. Her tiny fingers curled around her mother's hand, and her bright blue eyes sparkled with curiosity. They whispered promises of love and adventure, envisioning the wonderful life that lay ahead for their little girl.

As Sophie grew, it became clear that her connection to nature was extraordinary. She spent her early days exploring the garden, speaking to the flowers as if they were her friends. Each day, she would eagerly race outside, her laughter mingling with the songs of birds and the rustling leaves. The villagers often found her in the meadows, coaxing daisies to bloom or gathering wildflowers to create beautiful bouquets for her mother.

One sunny afternoon, while wandering through the forest, Sophie stumbled upon a hidden glade. Sunlight poured through the leaves, illuminating the area in a soft, golden hue. In the center stood a magnificent tree, its branches sprawling wide and its roots twisting deep into the earth. Sophie felt an inexplicable pull toward the tree, as if it were calling to her.

With her heart racing, she approached the ancient tree and placed her hand on its rough bark. Instantly, a warm energy coursed through her, filling her with a sense of peace and belonging. She closed her eyes, and in that moment, she could hear the whispers of the forest the rustling leaves, the chirping birds, and the distant babbling of a stream. It was as if the entire world was alive, sharing its secrets with her.

Sophie spent countless afternoons in that glade, forging a bond with the tree and the magical realm surrounding her. She felt a profound sense of purpose, knowing that she had a special connection to nature and the magic of Ravenrode. Little did she know that her journey was onlybeginning, and the friendships she would form would be the foundation of her adventures to come.

As her fifth birthday approached, the village buzzed with excitement, not just for Sophie's celebration but for the annual Festival of Blooms a cherished event honoring the beauty of nature. The villagers prepared for the festival, decorating the square with colorful flowers, ribbons, and lanterns that swayed gently in the breeze.

On the morning of her birthday, Sophie woke up to a chorus of birds singing outside her window. With a smile, she hopped out of bed and rushed to her parents, who greeted her with warm hugs and heartfelt wishes. "Today is your special day, my little flower!" her mother said, presenting her with a beautiful flower crown made of daisies and violets.

After the birthday breakfast, Sophie and her family made their way to the village square, where the festival was in full swing. Children played games, laughter echoed in the air, and the aroma of freshly baked treats wafted through the crowd. But Sophie's eyes were drawn to the flower display, which sparkled in the sunlight.

Suddenly, Sophie felt a tingle in her fingertips. She approached the display and knelt down to touch the flowers. As she did, a gentle breeze swept through the square, causing the petals to sway and dance. The villagers paused, watching in awe as the flowers bloomed even more vibrantly, their colors bursting with life.

The crowd erupted in applause, and Sophie's heart swelled with joy. She realized that her gift was not just a connection to nature, but a power to nurture and bring beauty to the world around her.

"Happy Birthday, Sophie!" the villagers cheered, and in that moment, she felt truly special part of a community that cherished her unique gifts.

As the festival continued, Sophie wandered through the crowd, her spirit soaring with happiness. It was on this day that she began to understand the importance of her connection to nature and the magical bond that would lead her to her lifelong friends.

Chapter 2

Leo's Quest for Adventure

As dawn broke in Ravenrode on the morning of Sophie's birthday, the village was stirred awake by the excited cries of animals and the warm rays of the sun. In a small, sunlit cottage located near the village square, Leo Anderson was born amidst a chorus of joyful laughter. His arrival into the world was heralded by the delightful chirping of birds outside, as if nature itself celebrated the birth of this spirited boy.

Leo's parents, Clara and James Anderson, were known for their adventurous spirits and love for exploration. As they gazed at their son, who was already squirming and reaching out with tiny fists, they felt a sense of excitement about the life that lay ahead for him. "He's going to be a handful!" Clara chuckled, her eyes sparkling with love.

From a young age, Leo showed an insatiable curiosity. He was a whirlwind of energy, always seeking new experiences. While other children might sit quietly, Leo would be the first to dash outside, ready to embark on an adventure. His heart raced at the thought of climbing trees, chasing after butterflies, or exploring the edges of the mystical forest that bordered their village.

The Spirit of Adventure

One sunny afternoon, just after Leo's third birthday, he ventured into the woods with his trusty companion, a scruffy little dog named Rusty. The two were inseparable, and together they discovered the hidden wonders of Ravenrode. They followed winding paths, leaped over babbling brooks, and chased sunbeams that filtered through the leaves.

On that day, Leo stumbled upon a secret clearing adorned with wildflowers and tall, whispering grasses. In the center stood a majestic oak tree, its broad branches stretching toward the sky. Leo felt an immediate connection to the tree, as if it were welcoming him into its embrace.

"Come on, Rusty!" he called, and together they dashed toward the tree. Leo gazed up, mesmerized by the way the sunlight danced through the leaves, casting playful shadows on the ground. He could already envision himself climbing the tree, reaching for the sky and feeling the thrill of freedom.

Without hesitation, Leo scrambled up the trunk, his heart pounding with excitement. As he climbed higher, he felt a rush of adrenaline, exhilarated by the view. From his perch, he could see the

entire village, the rooftops glistening in the sunlight, and the river winding like a silver ribbon through the landscape.

"Look, Rusty! We can see everything from up here!" he shouted, his voice echoing through the clearing. In that moment, Leo knew he was destined for adventure, a life filled with exploration and daring feats.

A Birthday Celebration

As the days passed, Leo's fifth birthday approached, and the village buzzed with excitement for the upcoming Festival

of Blooms. The entire community came together to prepare for the celebration, adorning the village square with colorful banners and fragrant flowers. The air was filled with laughter and the sweet scent of freshly baked treats.

On the morning of his birthday, Leo awoke to the sound of clattering pots and pans in the kitchen. "Happy Birthday, my little adventurer!" his mother exclaimed, presenting him with a bright blue bandana and a wooden sword, a gift that ignited his imagination.

"Thanks, Mom! This is perfect!" Leo grinned, tying the bandana around his head and striking a heroic pose with the sword. Today, he would be the bravest knight in Ravenrode, ready to take on any challenge.

After breakfast, Leo, accompanied by his parents, made his way to the village square. The energy in the air was electric as children ran about, playing games and laughing, while adults prepared for the festivities. Leo's eyes sparkled with delight as he took in the sights and sounds of the celebration.

When the time for the festival arrived, Leo joined his friends in a series of games and activities, from sack races to tug-of-war. He embraced the competitive spirit, often leading his team to victory with his boundless energy. With Rusty by his side, he felt unstoppable, laughing and cheering with his friends as they played.

A Special Moment

As the sun began to set, casting a warm golden glow over the village, a hush fell over the crowd. The villagers gathered in the square to witness the highlight of the festival the blooming ceremony. It was a cherished tradition where the oldest tree in Ravenrode, known as the Heartwood, was adorned with garlands of flowers, symbolizing unity and friendship among the villagers.

Leo felt a sense of excitement as he stood among his friends, ready to participate in the ceremony. As they gathered around the Heartwood, a wave of magic swept through the air. The flowers began to bloom with a vibrant display of colors, releasing a sweet fragrance that enveloped the crowd.

In that moment, Leo felt a deep connection to the people around him. He realized that he was part of something much larger an intricate tapestry of friendships and shared experiences that would shape his life. As the villagers celebrated

together, Leo knew that this was just the beginning of many adventures to come, and he was eager to embrace them all.

With his heart filled with joy and a sense of belonging, Leo turned to the villagers and shouted, "Let's make every day an adventure!"

Chapter 3

Maya and the Enchanted Sketchbook

As the sun dipped low on the horizon, painting the sky with hues of orange and pink, another child was born in the village of Ravenrode. Maya Thompson entered the world with a quiet grace, her arrival heralded by a gentle breeze that whispered through the trees. Her parents, Elizabeth and Oliver Thompson, were filled with wonder as they welcomed their daughter into their warm, cozy home.

From her earliest days, Maya exhibited a natural curiosity about the world around her. She had a keen eye for detail and an imaginative spirit that often led her on countless explorations. While other children played games, Maya could be found scribbling in her notebook, capturing the beauty of nature in intricate drawings and stories.

The Power of Imagination

Maya's most extraordinary gift was her ability to bring her drawings to life. With each stroke of her pencil, she could manifest the creatures and landscapes she imagined, making them real for a brief moment. This power was a closely guarded secret, known only to her family.

As she sat in her garden one afternoon, surrounded by colorful flowers and buzzing bees, Maya opened her notebook and began to sketch a beautiful butterfly. With each detail she added, the air shimmered with magic, and soon, the butterfly sprang to life, fluttering around her head. Maya's eyes widened in delight as she watched her creation dance among the blooms, its delicate wings reflecting the sunlight.

"Come back, little friend!" she called, reaching out her hand. The butterfly hovered for a moment before landing gently on her fingertip. Maya giggled, feeling a warm connection to the creature she had brought to life.

A Birthday Celebration

As Maya's fifth birthday approached, the excitement in Ravenrode reached a fever pitch with the Festival of Blooms.

The village square was adorned with colorful decorations, and families prepared for the joyful celebration. Maya could hardly contain her anticipation, dreaming of the festivities that awaited her.

On the morning of her birthday, Maya awoke to the sweet aroma of pancakes wafting through the house. Her parents greeted her with

warm hugs and presented her with a beautiful set of colored pencils and a new sketchbook. "May your imagination soar!" her mother exclaimed, her eyes sparkling with love.

After breakfast, Maya, bubbling with excitement, rushed to join her friends in the village square. As the festival unfolded, she reveled in the joy and laughter surrounding her. The square buzzed with life, as children ran about, participating in games and sharing treats, while musicians played lively tunes that filled the air.

An Unexpected Discovery

As the festivities continued, Maya wandered away from the crowd, drawn by the sound of rustling leaves in the nearby forest. She found a secluded spot near the edge of the woods, where sunlight filtered through the branches, casting a warm glow on the ground.

Curiosity sparked in her heart as she pulled out her sketchbook. Inspired by the beauty of her surroundings, Maya began to draw a magnificent tree with sprawling branches and intricate leaves.

As she sketched, she poured her imagination into the artwork, creating a mystical creature perched upon the branches a wise owl with shimmering feathers. To her astonishment, as she completed the final stroke, the owl blinked and came to life, taking flight and soaring into the sky. Maya gasped, her heart racing with excitement. "Come back!" she called, following the owl as it swooped gracefully through the trees.

The owl landed on a nearby branch, and Maya marveled at its beauty. "You're amazing!" she exclaimed, reaching out her hand. The owl tilted its head, as if acknowledging her words. In that moment, Maya realized her gift was not just a tool for her imagination; it was a bridge to connect her with the magic of the world.

The Blooming Ceremony

Later that evening, as the sun began to set, Maya joined the villagers gathered around the Heartwood tree for the blooming ceremony. The air buzzed with anticipation as the villagers decorated the tree with garlands of flowers, celebrating unity and friendship.

As the flowers began to bloom in response to the collective energy of the crowd, Maya felt a surge of magic wash over her. She closed her eyes, envisioning the wise owl perched on the branches of the Heartwood. As she opened her eyes, she noticed the owl had returned, perched high above, watching over the festivities.

In that moment, Maya understood the significance of her gift the ability to bring her imagination to life, not just for herself, but to inspire and connect with others. Surrounded by her friends and family, she felt a sense of belonging, knowing that this bond would lead her and her friends on countless adventures in the magical world of Ravenrode.

- 13 -

Chapter 4

The Windborne Hero

On the far edge of Ravenrode, nestled in a small house surrounded by rolling hills, Finn Parker was born on a stormy night. As the wind howled outside, lightning streaked across the sky, followed by the rumbling of thunder. But inside the Parker home, a calmness prevailed, as if the storm bowed in reverence to the newborn child. Finn's parents, Margaret and Henry Parker, held their baby close, sensing there was something special about him something different.

As Finn grew older, it became clear that he was not like other children. He had a quiet, contemplative nature, preferring to observe rather than participate. While his friends ran through the fields, chasing each other in endless games, Finn could often be found sitting on a hill, gazing out at the horizon, lost in thought.

The Quiet Storm

One particularly windy afternoon, when Finn was just four years old, he wandered to the top of his favorite hill, a place where he felt most at peace. The sky above was a swirling mass of clouds, and the wind tugged at his hair and clothes. Most children would have run for shelter, but Finn stood still, feeling the energy in the air.

As he stared at the sky, something incredible happened. The wind around him began to swirl, forming a small, controlled vortex that danced around his feet. Finn's eyes widened in awe as he realized the wind was responding to him moving with his thoughts, his emotions. He raised his hand, and the wind followed, spiraling upward, lifting leaves and dust into the air.

In that moment, Finn discovered his power the ability to manipulate air. It wasn't loud or flashy, but it was powerful in its quiet control, just like Finn himself.

From that day forward, Finn's connection with the wind deepened. He learned to call upon it in moments of need, using it to lift small objects, clear paths, or even carry messages across the village. But he kept his ability a secret, not out of fear, but because it felt personal like a conversation between him and the wind that only they understood.

A Mysterious Presence

As Finn's fifth birthday approached, the excitement in Ravenrode for the Festival of Blooms grew. But for Finn, the festival wasn't just about

the celebrations. It was a time when the magic in the air seemed stronger, when he could feel the pulse of the wind more keenly than ever before.

On the eve of his birthday, Finn ventured out into the woods, following a path that led him to a quiet clearing. The trees around him whispered softly, and the air was still, as if waiting. Finn closed his eyes and took a deep breath, feeling the wind stir in response.

Suddenly, a cool breeze brushed against his face, carrying with it the scent of rain and the sound of distant thunder. Finn opened his eyes to see the sky darkening, and in the distance, a figure stood at the edge of the clearing a tall man cloaked in shadow, his face obscured by the growing storm.

Before Finn could approach, the man vanished, disappearing into the storm. The wind settled, leaving Finn standing alone in the clearing, filled with questions. Who was the man? And why did Finn feel as though he was destined to meet him again?

Finn's heart raced, but he didn't feel fear. Instead, he felt drawn to the figure, as if they were connected somehow. The man raised his hand, and the wind swirled around them both, stronger now, more purposeful. Finn knew this figure was no ordinary person he was tied to the wind, just as Finn was.

A Birthday to Remember

The next day, Finn's birthday arrived, and with it came the vibrant energy of the Festival of Blooms. The village square was alive with color, music, and laughter, but Finn's mind was elsewhere on the mysterious figure in the woods and the growing connection he felt with the wind.

His parents gave him a simple gift: a small, hand-carved wooden whistle shaped like a bird. "For calling the wind," his father joked, but Finn felt the weight of the words. He smiled and thanked them, pocketing the whistle, knowing that he didn't need it to summon the wind the wind was already with him, always.

As Finn joined his friends in the village square, he noticed how the wind seemed to play around him, lifting strands of his hair and swirling gently at his feet. His friends laughed and played, unaware of the power Finn wielded just beneath the surface.

When the time for the blooming ceremony arrived, Finn stood with the villagers around the Heartwood tree, feeling the magic of the moment. As the flowers began to bloom, carried by the energy of the crowd, Finn felt the wind stir again, stronger this time, lifting the petals into the air.

Without thinking, he raised his hand, and the wind followed, carrying the petals higher and higher until they danced above the crowd, shimmering in the evening light. The villagers gasped in awe, unaware that it was Finn who had guided the wind.

As the petals finally drifted back down, Finn lowered his hand, a small smile playing on his lips. He was beginning to understand his place in the world a quiet force, like the wind, unnoticed but ever-present, ready to shape the future alongside his friends.

Chapter 5

The Shadows Speak

Nora Caldwell was born on a cold winter night in the heart of Ravenrode. The air was crisp, and the moon hung high in the sky, casting an eerie silver glow over the quiet village. In a small, ancient house at the edge of the forest, Nora took her first breath, her arrival marked by an unusual stillness. Her parents, Evelyn and Marcus Caldwell, held her close, sensing a strange, unexplainable presence around their newborn daughter.

From the moment she could walk, Nora displayed an uncanny ability to slip unnoticed into the background. She was quiet, observant, and often knew things that no one had told her. Her pale blue eyes seemed to see through people, as though she could peer into the hidden parts of their minds and souls. Ravenrode's elders would sometimes murmur about her, calling her "the girl with the knowing eyes."

But it wasn't until she turned five that Nora discovered the true extent of her gift a gift that would forever set her apart from the others.

Whispers in the Dark

One evening, just before her fifth birthday, Nora sat alone in her bedroom, the only light coming from a flickering candle on her bedside table. The shadows on the walls seemed to shift and move, as though alive. Nora had always felt drawn to the dark, to the places where light did not reach. But this night was different.

As she stared into the shadows, they began to whisper. The voices were faint at first, barely audible, but they grew louder with each passing moment. Nora didn't feel fear she felt curiosity. She leaned closer to the shadows, her heart beating steadily as she listened.

The whispers told her things. They spoke of secrets hidden beneath the earth, of places long forgotten by the people of Ravenrode. They whispered of ancient magic, of powers that lay dormant, waiting to be awakened. And they told her something else something that sent a chill down her spine.

The shadows spoke of danger. A darkness was coming, something that would threaten not just Ravenrode, but the entire world. And somehow, Nora was connected to it.

She closed her eyes, feeling the weight of the knowledge pressing down on her. The shadows had revealed something terrifying, but they had also given her a glimpse of her own power the ability to hear and speak with the dark, to know the secrets hidden in the shadows.

A Suspenseful Discovery

The next day, on the eve of her fifth birthday, Nora ventured into the forest that bordered her family's home. She often came here when she needed to think, to be alone. The trees seemed to whisper her name, and the shadows beneath the canopy felt familiar, like old friends.

As she walked deeper into the woods, Nora felt a strange pull, as if something or someone was guiding her. The path before her twisted and turned, leading her farther from the village and deeper into the unknown. The trees grew taller, their branches intertwining to form a natural archway above her head.

And then, she found it.

A small, ancient well, hidden deep within the forest. It was overgrown with ivy, and the stones were worn with age, but there was something unmistakably powerful about it. Nora approached cautiously, her heart pounding in her chest. As she peered over the edge of the well, the shadows seemed to swirl within, as though waiting for her.

Without thinking, Nora reached out her hand, and the shadows leapt from the well, wrapping themselves around her arm. But instead of fear, Nora felt a surge of energy a connection. The shadows whispered again, revealing secrets about the well, about the magic that lay beneath it.

And then they told her something else something more immediate.

"Someone is watching," they whispered.

Nora turned quickly, her eyes scanning the trees. At first, she saw nothing. But then, out of the corner of her eye, she caught a glimpse of movement a figure hidden in the shadows. Her heart raced. Was this the danger the shadows had warned her about? Or was it something else?

The figure remained still, watching her from the darkness. Nora could feel their gaze, heavy and intense, but they made no move to approach. After what felt like an eternity, the figure stepped back into the shadows and vanished.

The Festival of Blooms

Nora returned to the village that night, the strange encounter weighing heavily on her mind. Who had been watching her? And why? The shadows had warned her of danger, but they had also given her power. For the first time, Nora felt truly connected to the magic of the world around her.

The next day, her birthday arrived, and with it came the Festival of Blooms. As the villagers gathered in the square, Nora stayed on the outskirts, her eyes constantly scanning the crowd. She felt uneasy, as though the figure from the forest could appear at any moment.

When it came time for the blooming ceremony, Nora stood with her friends, Sophie, Leo, Finn, and Maya, beneath the towering Heartwood tree. The flowers bloomed in vibrant colors, and the village cheered, but Nora felt distant, her mind still caught in the shadows.

As the petals floated down from the tree, carried by the wind that Finn had summoned, Nora closed her eyes and reached out with her mind, searching the shadows for answers. And then she heard it the whisper she had been dreading.

"He is coming."

Nora's eyes snapped open, and she looked at Finn, her heart pounding. The shadows had revealed the truth to her the danger was real, and it was coming for them. But there was something else, too something she hadn't expected.

Finn Parker, her quiet, contemplative friend, was at the center of it all. He was the key to the mystery, the one who would either save them or lead them into darkness.

Nora felt a chill run down her spine. The shadows had spoken. Now it was up to her to protect her friends, even if it meant delving deeper into the dark powers that whispered in her ear.

Chapter 6

The Gathering Storm

As the Festival of Blooms continued in Ravenrode, a palpable tension hung in the air, unseen by most but deeply felt by those who were attuned to the magic that flowed through the village. Finn, Maya, Leo, and Nora stood together, watching the petals fall like confetti around them, their minds racing with the revelations of the past few days.

Finn glanced at Nora, who seemed lost in thought, her brow furrowed. He could sense her unease, and it made him anxious. What had the shadows revealed to her? What danger were they facing? He felt a strange connection to her, as if their fates were intertwined in ways he could not yet comprehend.

"Hey, Nora," Finn said softly, trying to break through her contemplation. "Are you okay?"

Nora snapped back to the present, her eyes meeting his. "I I'm fine. Just thinking," she replied, her voice barely above a whisper. But Finn knew better; the shadows had told her something, and he felt the weight of her silence pressing down on them both.

Suddenly, a loud cheer erupted from the crowd, pulling their attention back to the festival. The villagers danced and laughed, oblivious to the brewing storm that hung just beyond the horizon. Finn watched as Leo joined in the festivities, his carefree spirit shining brightly. Maya, too, was caught up in the joy, sketching the scene with fervor, her imagination spilling onto the pages of her notebook.

But Finn and Nora remained on the outskirts, feeling the tension that no one else seemed to notice.

The Dark Figure Returns

As the sun dipped below the horizon, casting long shadows across the village, a sudden chill swept through the square. Finn shivered, and Nora instinctively stepped closer to him. "Did you feel that?" she asked, her voice low.

"Yeah," Finn replied, scanning the area. "It's like the wind changed."

Then, without warning, the figure from the woods appeared at the edge of the square. Cloaked in darkness, he stood there, a silhouette against the dying light. The laughter and music faded into silence as the villagers sensed something amiss.

Finn's heart raced. "Who is that?" he murmured, glancing at Nora. She was watching the figure intently, her eyes wide with recognition.

"I don't know," she whispered, "but I think he's the one I saw in the forest."

The figure took a step forward, and as he did, a gust of wind swept through the square, scattering petals and sending shivers down everyone's spines. "I have come to warn you," the figure said, his voice deep and resonant, echoing with power.

A Warning Unfolds

The villagers watched, captivated and fearful, as the figure continued, "Darkness approaches Ravenrode, and you Finn Parker must be prepared. The balance of power is shifting, and only you can hold it together."

Finn felt a surge of confusion and fear. Why was this figure singling him out? He could feel the weight of the villagers' gazes upon him, their hopes and fears resting on his shoulders.

"What do you mean?" Finn called out, stepping forward. "What darkness? How can I help?"

The figure raised a hand, and the wind intensified, swirling around Finn like a protective shield. "Listen closely, Finn. The shadows have awakened, and they are searching for their master. You are connected to the wind, but it is the shadows that will test your strength. You must gather your friends Maya, Leo, and Nora. Together, you will face the storm."

Before Finn could respond, the figure turned and vanished into the night, leaving behind a lingering chill and a sense of urgency. The villagers murmured amongst themselves, confusion and concern etched on their faces.

The Call to Action

Finn looked at Nora, who was pale, her eyes reflecting the fear that had taken root in her heart. "Nora, what did the shadows tell you?" he pressed gently, determined to understand what they were up against.

Nora took a deep breath, her voice trembling. "They told me something dark is coming, Finn. Something that will try to separate us. We have to stick together, no matter what."

Finn nodded, a sense of resolve washing over him. He could feel the wind shifting, as if urging him to take action. "We need to gather the others. If the shadows are really after us, we can't wait any longer."

As they made their way through the village, Finn felt the weight of his newfound responsibility. The villagers had always looked up to him, but now it felt different. He was no longer just a boy; he was becoming a leader, a protector of his friends and their home.

They found Leo and Maya still reveling in the festivities, laughter echoing through the square. But as Finn approached, he could see their joy fading. "Guys, we need to talk," he said, urgency lacing his tone.

Leo's playful demeanor shifted instantly. "What's going on?" he asked, concern replacing the laughter in his eyes.

"We're in danger," Finn said, glancing at Nora before continuing. "A figure from the woods just warned us. Something dark is coming, and we need to be prepared."

Maya's eyes widened, and she looked at Finn with determination. "What can we do?"

Finn took a deep breath, grounding himself in the moment. "We need to stick together and face whatever comes our way. The figure said we'll need each other to confront the shadows."

The Promise of Unity

The friends exchanged glances, a silent understanding passing between them. They were bound by their experiences, their powers, and their friendship. They would stand together against whatever darkness threatened Ravenrode.

As the festival continued around them, Finn felt a newfound strength surging within him, a resolve to protect those he loved. The wind rustled through the trees, a reminder of the power he could wield.

"Let's meet at my house tonight," Finn suggested. "We can talk more and figure out our next steps."Nora nodded, her expression fierce. "We won't let the darkness win. Together, we're stronger."

And so, under the watchful gaze of the moon and stars, the four friends made a promise no matter what challenges lay ahead, they would face them united, ready to embrace their destinies as guardians of Ravenrode.

Chapter 7

The Five Reunite

The night had grown deeper, the air heavy with the weight of the unknown, as Finn, Nora, Leo, and Maya gathered at Finn's house. The fire in the hearth crackled softly, casting dancing shadows on the walls, but the warmth did little to ease the tension that hung in the room. The danger that loomed over Ravenrode was real, and they all knew that the time for action was fast approaching.

However, one of them was missing.

Sophie Bennett, the heart of their group, had been strangely distant in recent weeks. It wasn't like her to avoid them, and Finn felt a growing concern in his chest. He had always been able to count on Sophie's intuition and calm presence, but something had changed. Ever since the strange happenings began, Sophie had seemed... different. As if she knew something she wasn't ready to share.

Finn paced the room, his thoughts racing. "We can't do this without her," he said, looking at the others. "Sophie's always been the one to hold us together. We need her."

Nora nodded, her gaze distant as she listened to the flickers of shadow in the room. "The shadows haven't mentioned Sophie, but I can feel something... like she's dealing with something on her own."

Maya, who was usually full of energy, sat quietly by the fire, sketching out symbols in the air with her finger. She glanced at Finn. "Do you think she's in trouble?"

Leo, always the optimist, leaned back in his chair. "Maybe she's just taking some time to think. You know how she is she likes to figure things out before she says anything."

But Finn wasn't convinced. Sophie had never kept secrets from them before. Something was wrong, and they couldn't afford to wait any longer.

"We need to find her," Finn said decisively. "Tonight."

Sophie's Secret

The group set out into the night, the wind whispering through the trees as they made their way toward Sophie's house. The village was quiet, with most of the townspeople having retired after the festival. Only the occasional flicker of lanterns in windows provided any light as they walked through the narrow streets.

When they reached Sophie's house, they found it dark, the curtains drawn tightly over the windows. Finn's heart sank. He knew Sophie's parents were out of town for the week, and she was supposed to be home alone, but the house felt too still, too silent.

"I'll check around back," Leo said, moving quickly without waiting for a response.

Finn knocked on the door, the sound echoing in the quiet night. No answer. He knocked again, louder this time. Still nothing.

"Maybe she's not here," Maya said softly, though her tone was laced with doubt.

But Finn wasn't giving up. He tried the door handle, and to his surprise, it turned easily in his hand. The door creaked open, revealing the darkened hallway inside.

"I don't like this," Nora whispered, standing close to Finn as they stepped inside. "Something feels... off."

The house was eerily quiet as they entered. The familiar scent of lavender, which always filled Sophie's home, was gone, replaced by the cold scent of night air. Finn felt a knot tighten in his chest.

"Sophie?" Finn called out, his voice echoing through the empty space.

They moved through the house, checking each room, but there was no sign of her. It was as though Sophie had simply vanished. Then, as they entered the living room, Nora suddenly froze.

"Wait," she whispered, her voice urgent. "I hear something."

The others stopped, listening. At first, there was only silence, but then... a faint humming, almost like a lullaby, drifted from upstairs.

"That's Sophie," Finn said, his heart leaping. He recognized the melody. It was an old tune that Sophie's mother used to sing to her when they were children. He hadn't heard it in years.

They hurried up the stairs, the humming growing louder with each step. When they reached Sophie's room, they found the door slightly ajar. Finn hesitated for a moment, then pushed it open.

There, sitting in the middle of the room, was Sophie. Her back was to them, and she was humming softly to herself, her body swaying gently to the rhythm of the song. Around her, strange symbols were drawn on the floor in a circle, glowing faintly in the dim light.

"Sophie?" Finn said, his voice shaking slightly. "What's going on?"

Sophie didn't turn around. She continued to hum, as if she hadn't heard him.

Finn stepped forward, but Nora grabbed his arm, pulling him back. "Wait," she said, her voice filled with warning. "Something's not right. Look at the symbols."

Finn's eyes dropped to the floor, and his stomach churned. The symbols were unlike anything he had ever seen twisting, ancient markings that seemed to pulse with a dark energy. Nora knelt beside them, her hand hovering just above the ground as she listened to the shadows.

"She's... trapped," Nora whispered, her face pale. "But not by anyone else. She did this herself."

Finn felt a cold dread creep through him. "Why would she trap herself?"Nora shook her head. "I don't know. But whatever it is, it's powerful. And dangerous."

Breaking the Circle

"We have to help her," Maya said, stepping forward, determination in her eyes. "Whatever this is, Sophie wouldn't do this unless she had a reason."

Leo nodded in agreement. "We've faced worse before, right? We just need to figure out how to break the circle."

Nora frowned, still listening to the whispers that only she could hear. "It's not that simple. This magic... it's ancient. Sophie must have found something, something powerful, and now it's consuming her."

Finn's heart pounded in his chest. "Then we'll do whatever it takes. We can't lose her."

Together, they knelt around the circle, their hands hovering over the symbols. Finn closed his eyes, calling upon the wind, hoping it would guide him as it always had. He could feel its gentle push, urging him forward, and as the breeze swept through the room, the symbols flickered.

Nora placed her hand on one of the symbols, her voice low as she spoke to the shadows. "Sophie, we're here. You need to come back to us."

For a moment, nothing happened. Then, slowly, Sophie's humming stopped. She blinked, as if waking from a deep sleep, and turned to look at them. Her eyes were filled with a mixture of confusion and fear.

"Finn?" she whispered. "What... what happened?"

Finn let out a breath he hadn't realized he was holding. "We don't know, but you're safe now. We're here."

Sophie's eyes welled with tears, and she reached out to him. "I was trying to protect you," she said, her voice trembling. "I found something something dark and I didn't want it to hurt any of you."

Finn took her hand, pulling her close. "We're in this together, Sophie. No more secrets."

The symbols on the floor began to fade, their glow dimming until they disappeared entirely. The air in the room grew lighter, the oppressive weight lifting as Sophie's self-imposed prison crumbled.

Nora stood, her expression still guarded. "There's more to this, Sophie. Whatever you found, it's connected to the danger we've been sensing."

Sophie nodded, wiping away her tears. "I know. And now that we're all together... we'll face it. But I need to show you something first."

The five friends exchanged a look of determination. Together, they would uncover the mystery that had drawn them into this darkness. They would face the coming storm not as individuals, but as a united force, stronger than ever.

Chapter 8

The Hidden Truth

Sophie stood in the center of her room, still shaken but resolute. Her friends circled around her, their eyes filled with concern and questions. Finn held her hand tightly, offering a quiet assurance, while Nora studied the remnants of the symbols that had faded from the floor, still wary of what Sophie had encountered.

"I didn't mean to keep this from you," Sophie began, her voice soft but steady. "I thought if I could figure it out on my own, I could protect all of you. But I was wrong."

Maya, always the first to support her friends, stepped closer. "We don't blame you, Sophie. But we need to understand what's happening. What did you find?"

Sophie took a deep breath, gathering her thoughts. "It started a few weeks ago, after the first signs of the strange things happening around Ravenrode the disappearing animals, the whispers in the woods. I felt something pulling me, like a voice in the back of my mind, guiding me to a place I had never been before."

Leo frowned, crossing his arms. "Where did it lead you?"

"To the forest," Sophie replied, her eyes darting to the window as if the memory still haunted her. "There's an old clearing deep in the woods, a place I've never seen before. It's hidden, like it's been forgotten by time. But when I got there, I found something buried beneath the earth an ancient book."

"A book?" Finn echoed, his curiosity piqued.

Sophie nodded. "Not just any book. It's filled with magic dark magic. Spells that I've never seen, not in any of the books we've studied. I knew it was dangerous the moment I touched it, but something compelled me to bring it back. I thought I could keep it safe, that I could learn from it without falling into its power."Nora's eyes narrowed as she listened.

"That's why you created the circle," she said, gesturing to where the symbols had been. "You were trying to contain the magic."

"Yes," Sophie confirmed. "But the more I studied it, the more it consumed me. I could feel it seeping into my thoughts, changing me. That's when I realized I couldn't handle it alone. The book it's not just powerful, it's alive."

The Unveiling

The room fell silent as Sophie's words sank in. Finn felt a chill run down his spine. A living book of dark magic? This was beyond anything they had ever faced before. He tightened his grip on Sophie's hand, the weight of the situation settling on him.

"We need to see this book," Finn said, determination in his voice. "If it's as dangerous as you say, we need to understand what we're dealing with."

Sophie hesitated, but then she nodded. "It's in my room, hidden under the floorboards. I thought it was safest there."

She led them to a small, unassuming rug in the corner of her room. With a quick glance at the others, Sophie knelt down and carefully pulled back the rug, revealing a loose floorboard underneath. She lifted it, and there, resting in the hollow space, was the book.

It was old ancient, even. The leather cover was cracked and worn, with strange symbols etched into it that seemed to pulse faintly in the dim light. The edges of the pages were blackened, as if they had been singed by fire. The air around it felt charged, like a storm about to break.

Finn stared at the book, feeling the pull of its power. "This is it?" he asked, his voice barely above a whisper.

Sophie nodded. "I've only read a few pages, but every spell is more dangerous than the last. It talks about controlling the elements, summoning shadows, bending time itself. But there's one spell in particular... one that I think is the key to all of this."Nora leaned in, her eyes dark and focused. "What kind of spell?"

Sophie swallowed hard. "It's a spell to awaken something ancient, something that's been sleeping beneath Ravenrode for centuries. The book doesn't say exactly what it is, but it calls it 'The Darkness.'"

The room grew colder at Sophie's words. Finn felt the wind stir slightly around him, a reminder of the power that flowed through him. "The Darkness?" he repeated, his voice tense. "What does that mean?"

"I don't know," Sophie admitted, her voice shaking. "But I think someone or something is trying to awaken it. And if they succeed, Ravenrode will be the first to fall."

A Plan Unfolds

Maya stepped forward, her mind racing. "We need to stop it. We can't let this Darkness wake up, whatever it is. But how do we even begin?"

Leo, always the strategist, rubbed his chin thoughtfully. "We need more information. If the book was buried, there might be more to this story. Something the village has forgotten. Maybe the Elders know."

"Or the archives," Nora added, her voice steady. "There are old records in the village archives, hidden histories that most people don't even remember. If there's a connection between Ravenrode and this Darkness, it could be there."

Finn nodded, feeling a sense of purpose growing within him. "We'll split up. Leo and Maya, you two head to the Elders. See if they know anything about this ancient magic or the Darkness. Nora, you and I will go to the archives. If there's anything written about this in the village's past, we'll find it."

"And what about me?" Sophie asked, her voice tinged with uncertainty.

Finn turned to her, his eyes full of trust. "You're coming with us. You know this magic better than anyone. We'll need your help to decipher anything we find."

Sophie nodded, though Finn could still see the doubt lingering in her eyes. She was scared of what she had uncovered and what it might mean for all of them. But she was also brave, and Finn knew she would stand by them, no matter what.

"We meet back here in a few hours," Finn said, looking around at his friends. "Whatever we find, we'll face it together."

The Shadows Stir

As they prepared to leave, a gust of wind rattled the windows, and the shadows in the corners of the room seemed to shift, as if alive. Nora's eyes flicked to the darkened corners, her expression tense.

"We're running out of time," she whispered. "The shadows are moving. Whatever's coming... it's close."

Finn felt the weight of her words settle on him. The wind outside howled, echoing his own sense of urgency. They needed answers and fast.

As the five friends left Sophie's house and split into their groups, Finn couldn't shake the feeling that they were on the edge of something far bigger than any of them had imagined. The storm was coming, and they would either face it united or be swept away by the Darkness that lurked just beyond the horizon.

Chapter 9

The Search for Answers

The wind carried a familiar chill as Finn, Nora, and Sophie walked through the winding streets of Ravenrode. It was late, and the village was quiet, but the three friends were wide awake, their minds racing with the weight of the new knowledge Sophie had shared.

"I still can't believe we've come this far," Nora said, her voice breaking the silence as they approached the edge of the village. "We were just kids when all of this started... and now, here we are."

Finn smiled softly. "Yeah, we're not so little anymore." He glanced at the reflection of the three of them in a nearby window. They had grown, not just in height but in strength. Ten years old now, the memories of their earlier adventures seemed both close and distant at the same time. Their bond was stronger than ever, but the mysteries surrounding them had only deepened.

Sophie nodded, though her expression remained serious. "It feels like it all started yesterday, but somehow, everything feels... bigger now. More dangerous." Her eyes darted between the streets, as though half expecting to see shadows moving in the darkness.

The weight of their age hung in the air 10 years old and facing things far beyond what children were meant to deal with. Finn could feel the pull of responsibility, the need to protect his friends from whatever dark force was awakening beneath Ravenrode.

Reaching the Archives

The village archives loomed ahead of them, an old stone building that had stood for centuries. It was a place few villagers visited anymore, but for Finn and his friends, it had become a treasure trove of forgotten knowledge. If there were answers to be found about the ancient Darkness Sophie had uncovered, they would find them here.

As they approached the entrance, Finn glanced at Nora, whose sharp eyes scanned the shadows. Her power the ability to hear and sense things others couldn't was growing stronger, just like his. The wind around them whispered secrets, and Finn felt it tugging at him, urging him to move faster.

"We should be careful," Nora whispered. "The shadows feel... different tonight."

Sophie gave a small nod, pulling her cloak tighter around her shoulders as the cold air seeped through the cracks of the night.

The archives were dimly lit by old lanterns, casting flickering shadows along the walls. The rows of books and scrolls, lined in perfect order, carried with them the weight of centuries. It was a place of secrets both forgotten and hidden.

They moved quickly, each step echoing through the empty halls. Finn led the way, his eyes scanning the spines of ancient books as they passed. They needed to find any records that mentioned the Darkness Sophie had spoken of, any connection to the magic that had been buried for so long.

The Forgotten Records

After several minutes of searching, they found a large, dusty tome hidden in the back corner of the archives. Its cover was worn and the pages yellowed, but the title was clear: *The Lost Histories of Ravenrode.*

"This has to be it," Finn said, carefully pulling the book from its shelf.

They gathered around a small table, and Sophie opened the book, her fingers trembling slightly. As she flipped through the pages, the text revealed stories of ancient magic, forgotten rituals, and strange occurrences that had shaped the village's past.

"Look," Sophie said, pointing to a passage written in fading ink.

"In the forest deep, a force sleeps a darkness bound by the magic of the old. It stirs only when the earth shifts and

the stars align. Beware the one who awakens it, for they hold the key to its release."

Nora leaned in closer, her brow furrowed. "That sounds exactly like what we're dealing with. The Darkness Sophie found it's been sleeping all this time."

Finn's heart pounded in his chest. They were so close to understanding, but they still didn't know who or what was trying to awaken this force. And more importantly, they didn't know how to stop it.

"There has to be more," Finn said, flipping through the pages as fast as he could without damaging the fragile book.

But before they could find anything further, the sound of footsteps echoed through the archives.

They froze.

Nora's eyes widened. "Someone's coming."

An Unexpected Visitor

The door to the archives creaked open, and a tall figure stepped inside. The flickering lanterns cast long shadows across the room, making it impossible to see the intruder's face clearly at first. Finn instinctively moved closer to Sophie, his protective instincts kicking in.

As the figure stepped into the light, they recognized him immediately Elder Rowan, one of the oldest and most mysterious members of the village council.

"What are you doing here at this hour?" Elder Rowan's voice was low, carrying both curiosity and suspicion.

Finn swallowed hard but stood his ground. "We're looking for answers," he said, his voice steady. "There's something happening in Ravenrode something dark. And we think it has to do with the ancient magic buried here."

Elder Rowan's expression softened slightly, though his eyes remained cautious. "You are still so young," he murmured, shaking his head. "Too young to be meddling in these matters."

"We're not children anymore," Nora said firmly, stepping forward. "We're ten years old now, and we've been facing these mysteries our whole lives. We deserve to know the truth."

Elder Rowan sighed deeply, as though the weight of the village's history rested on his shoulders alone. "Perhaps you are right," he said quietly. "But the truth is not an easy burden to carry. The Darkness you seek it is older than you can imagine, older than this village, older than the forest itself."

Finn felt a chill run down his spine. "Then tell us how to stop it," he urged. "Before it's too late."

Rowan hesitated, his gaze shifting between the three friends. "I will tell you what I know," he said at last. "But you must understand that once you start down this path, there is no turning back. You are not just children of Ravenrode anymore. You are guardians of its future."

Chapter 10

The Guardians of Ravenrode

The three friends stood frozen, Elder Rowan's words hanging heavily in the air. Guardians of Ravenrode? It felt both empowering and terrifying. They had always been different drawn to the mysteries that surrounded them but now, their role in the village's fate was undeniable.

Sophie shifted uncomfortably, the ancient book still resting in her hands. "What do you mean, guardians? Why us?"

Elder Rowan's weathered face softened with a hint of sorrow. "The village has a long history with forces that most would prefer to forget. Magic has always existed here, hidden beneath the surface. There have been many who, like you, were called to protect Ravenrode. But the time has come for new guardians to rise. You are connected to this place in ways you cannot yet understand. Each of you was chosen before you were born."

Nora exchanged a look with Finn, her eyes filled with both fear and resolve. "Chosen? By whom?"

"By the magic itself," Elder Rowan replied, his voice low but certain. "The village protects its own. It knows when danger is near, and it has given each of you a gift a power to fight the darkness that threatens to rise."

Finn's mind raced as he processed Rowan's words. "Guardians" chosen to protect Ravenrode from the darkness. It explained the strange abilities they had each begun to manifest, powers that had become stronger over the years. But it also meant they were about to face something far more dangerous than they had ever imagined.

Sophie, still holding the book, took a hesitant step forward. "If we're the guardians, then we need to know how to stop this Darkness. What's in this book... it feels like a part of the puzzle, but I don't know if it's the answer."

Elder Rowan's gaze fell on the ancient book, and for a moment, his eyes flashed with something unreadable fear, perhaps, or recognition. "That book," he whispered, "should never have been unearthed."

Sophie's hands tightened on the book's cover. "But it holds the key to understanding what's happening, doesn't it? I've already seen things inside that talk about awakening something beneath the village."

Rowan nodded solemnly. "Yes. The Darkness lies beneath Ravenrode, but it was sealed away long ago by the very magic that now protects you. The book holds ancient spells, some of which are far too dangerous for anyone especially someone so young to wield. But there may be clues within its pages about how to strengthen the seal."

Finn's heart pounded as the weight of their task began to sink in. They weren't just hunting for answers anymore they were facing an ancient evil that could destroy everything they had ever known. And now, at just ten years old, they were the ones standing between Ravenrode and its destruction.

"We're going to need more than just clues," Finn said, his voice steadier than he felt. "If this Darkness is trying to break free, we need to know how to stop it completely."

Rowan studied Finn for a long moment before finally nodding. "Then it's time you learned the truth about your powers. The strength you each possess isn't just magic. It's tied to the very essence of Ravenrode, to the elements that surround us. Finn, your connection to the wind is deeper than you realize. Nora, your ability to sense things others cannot comes from the earth itself. And Sophie... your gift is tied to light and shadow, to the balance between them."

Sophie's eyes widened in surprise. "Light and shadow?"

"Yes," Rowan continued. "You are all connected to the forces that protect this village. But it's up to you to learn how to use your gifts. The powers you possess will be the only thing strong enough to hold back the Darkness."

A Dangerous Path

Sophie closed the book, the weight of Elder Rowan's words pressing down on her. They were the guardians, bound to Ravenrode by magic older than anything they had imagined. But knowing that didn't make their task any easier. If anything, it made it even more daunting.

"What about the others?" Finn asked, glancing at Nora. "Leo and Maya are they part of this too?"

Elder Rowan nodded. "Each of you has a role to play. The five of you are stronger together than apart. Leo's strength and Maya's mind are just as crucial as your magic. The balance of power rests with all of you."

Nora crossed her arms, her mind racing. "So what do we do now? If this Darkness is waking up, we can't just sit around and wait for it to attack."

Rowan's eyes darkened. "You need to find the source. The seals that were placed on the Darkness are weakening, and you need to strengthen them before it's too late. There's a place deep within the forest, hidden from the eyes of most. It's called the Heart of Ravenrode. That is where the original seal was cast. If you can reach it, you may be able to stop the Darkness from rising."

Finn felt a rush of determination. It was a dangerous path, but it was the only way to protect the village and his friends. "We'll find it," he said firmly. "Whatever it takes."

Rowan looked at them with a mixture of pride and sadness. "Be careful, Finn. The Heart of Ravenrode is not an easy place to find. And once you're there, the magic protecting it is as dangerous as the Darkness itself. You'll need to rely on each other more than ever."

Sophie glanced at Finn, her eyes filled with both fear and hope. "We're in this together, right?"

Finn nodded, the wind stirring faintly around him. "Always."

A New Journey Begins

As they left the archives, the weight of their task settled heavily on their shoulders. The village was quiet, but Finn could feel the tension in the air the storm was coming, and they were running out of time.

They needed to gather their friends, prepare for the journey ahead. The Heart of Ravenrode was waiting for them, and with it, the answers they so desperately needed. But Finn couldn't shake the feeling that the Darkness was watching them, waiting for the right moment to strike.

"Do you think we can do this?" Sophie asked quietly as they walked through the dark streets.

Finn glanced at her, his heart steady. "We have to."

The five friends were destined for something greater, something dangerous. But they were ready. The guardians of Ravenrode would face whatever came their way.

And together, they would protect their home from the shadows threatening to swallow it whole.

Chapter 11

Awakening the Elements

The weight of the task ahead loomed over the group, but as they walked through the quiet village, an unspoken understanding formed between them. They had been chosen, not by chance, but by something ancient and powerful something that recognized the magic within each of them. And now, it was time to embrace that magic, to awaken the full extent of their powers.

As the wind rustled through the trees, Finn felt it stir within him, a familiar sensation that he was only beginning to understand. The others seemed deep in thought, each grappling with the reality of what they had just learned.

The group stopped by the edge of the woods, the moonlight casting long shadows across the clearing. Finn turned to his friends, his voice steady but filled with purpose. "If we're going to stop this Darkness, we need to figure out how to control our powers really control them. We can't just rely on instinct anymore."

Nora nodded, her eyes glinting with determination. "Elder Rowan said our powers are tied to Ravenrode itself. We need to understand what that means."

Sophie, holding the ancient book tightly against her chest, looked uncertain but resolute. "And we need to do it fast. I can feel the magic stirring inside me more than ever before. If I don't learn how to control it..." Her voice trailed off, fear flickering in her eyes.

Maya stepped forward, ever the planner. "We should each focus on our strengths. Finn, you've always had a connection with the wind. Maybe if you concentrate, you can push it further, see what else it can do."

Finn hesitated for a moment, but then he took a deep breath and nodded. The wind had always been there for him, a constant companion gentle when he needed calm, fierce when he was angry or afraid. But it had been more than that recently.

He could feel the air bending to his will, responding to his emotions in ways that seemed impossible.

He stepped forward, closing his eyes as he focused on the cool night breeze swirling around him. At first, it was subtle just a soft rustling of the leaves but then, as he reached deeper into himself, he felt the wind begin to change. It picked up speed, circling him faster and faster until it became a gust, whipping through the clearing with a force that surprised even him.

Maya gasped, taking a step back as the wind intensified. "Finn, that's... incredible."

Finn opened his eyes, watching as the trees bent slightly under the force of the wind. He could feel it now, really feel it like the air was an extension of himself, something he could bend and shape. With a focused thought, he willed the wind to calm, and just as quickly as it had come, the breeze slowed to a gentle whisper.

Nora raised an eyebrow, impressed. "Looks like you're getting the hang of it."

Finn smiled, though there was still a trace of awe in his expression. "It feels... natural. Like the wind's always been there, waiting for me to notice."

Sophie stepped forward, looking both determined and apprehensive. "If Finn can do that, maybe I can figure out more about my own power." She hesitated, glancing down at the book in her hands. "But light and shadow... I'm not sure where to even start."

Maya offered a reassuring smile. "We'll figure it out together. Try focusing on what you feel when the shadows move. You've always had a way of sensing things we can't."

Sophie nodded, taking a deep breath as she turned her attention to the shadows cast by the moonlight. She had always noticed them, the way they seemed to shift and stretch in ways that defied logic. And now, as she focused, she felt it again that strange pull between light and darkness, like two sides of the same coin.

Closing her eyes, Sophie willed herself to feel the connection. Slowly, she lifted her hand, and to her amazement, the shadows in the clearing began to respond. At first, it was subtle a slight shift in their shape but then, as she concentrated harder, they moved with more purpose, swirling together like a living entity.

The others watched in awe as the shadows gathered at Sophie's feet, forming into a solid shape a tendril of darkness that writhed and flickered like a flame. But just as quickly as it had formed, Sophie's concentration faltered, and the shadows dispersed, melting back into the night.

She staggered back, breathing heavily. "I I did it," she whispered, her voice filled with a mixture of wonder and fear.

Finn stepped forward, placing a reassuring hand on her shoulder. "You did. And you'll get stronger. We all will."

Nora, who had been quietly observing, stepped forward next. "My connection is with the earth," she said, her voice steady. "I've always felt it, even when I was little. The way the ground speaks to me, the way I can feel things before they happen."

She knelt down, placing her hands on the ground. Closing her eyes, Nora focused on the earth beneath her fingers. At first, nothing seemed to happen, but then, slowly, the ground began to hum with energy. It was subtle, like a heartbeat, but as Nora concentrated, the hum grew louder.

The earth responded to her touch, a gentle tremor spreading through the soil. And then, with a quiet crack, a small vine pushed its way up from the ground, curling around her fingers as if it were alive.

Nora smiled softly, her connection to the earth stronger than ever. "It's always been there," she said quietly. "The earth... it listens."

Maya, always the analytical one, stepped forward next. "My power might not be as visible as yours, but I know it's there. My mind, the way I can figure things out so quickly it's more than just intelligence. I can feel it, like I'm connected to patterns, to possibilities."

She closed her eyes, focusing inward. The others watched as Maya's face relaxed, her breathing slow and even. Suddenly, she opened her eyes, a glimmer of insight flashing in them. "I see it," she whispered, her voice filled with certainty. "The way forward. We need to head to the heart of the forest, but we can't go in blind. There's a pattern we have to follow."

Leo, always the last to step into the spotlight, finally spoke. "And I'll be the one to keep us safe when we get there. I may not have magic like the rest of you, but I've always known how to protect the people I care about. That's my gift."

United by Magic

Finn looked around at his friends, a sense of pride swelling in his chest. They had always been strong, but now, united by their magic, they were unstoppable. Each of them had a role to play, a unique power that would guide them in the days to come.

"We're ready," Finn said, his voice filled with confidence. "Whatever's waiting for us in the Heart of Ravenrode, we'll face it together."

The wind stirred once more, carrying with it the scent of the forest and the promise of the journey ahead. The guardians had awakened their powers, but their greatest test was still to come.

And together, they would face the Darkness that threatened to destroy everything they held dear.

Chapter 12

The Training Arena – Wind's Whisper

After their realization that their powers were far more potent than they had ever imagined, the group decided they needed a place to practice, somewhere secluded and away from prying eyes. Maya had used her power of pattern recognition to guide them deep into the forest, to a hidden clearing that felt ancient and powerful.

The clearing was surrounded by towering trees that formed a natural wall, their branches intertwining to create a canopy that blocked out the harsh sunlight, allowing only soft beams to filter through. The air was cool and calm, and there was an energy here, a pulse that seemed to hum beneath the ground. It was a perfect place to train, a sanctuary hidden from the outside world.

Finn stepped into the center of the clearing, the others watching from the edges. He could feel the wind stirring around him, eager to move at his command. This was the first real test of his abilities the first time he would push himself to see what he was truly capable of.

"I'm ready," Finn said, his voice filled with determination.

Leo, who had taken on the role of keeping them grounded and safe, nodded. "Take it slow, Finn. We're just figuring things out."

Finn closed his eyes and took a deep breath, letting the familiar sensation of the wind wash over him. He had always felt a connection to the air, a sense that it was alive, responding to his emotions. But now, after learning the truth about their powers, he knew that this connection went deeper than he had ever imagined.

Slowly, he raised his hands, palms open to the sky. The wind responded immediately, swirling around him in gentle currents. It was easy at first just a simple breeze but as Finn concentrated, he pushed harder, willing the air to move faster.

The wind obeyed, whipping around him in a spiraling vortex, the leaves on the ground swirling into the air. Finn could feel the power building inside him, like a storm waiting to be unleashed. His heart raced as he focused, pushing the wind to its limits.

With a sudden burst of energy, Finn flung his hands forward, and the wind exploded outward, a powerful gust that sent the leaves scattering and the trees swaying. The force of it surprised even him, and he staggered back, breathless but exhilarated.

Maya and Nora clapped from the sidelines, impressed. "You're getting the hang of it," Maya said with a grin. "But can you control it when it's more intense?"

Finn nodded, eager to push himself further. "I'm going to try something bigger," he said, his voice filled with determination.

He planted his feet firmly on the ground, closing his eyes once more. This time, he imagined the wind not as a gentle breeze, but as a force of nature powerful and untamed. He could feel the air around him stirring, responding to his thoughts. The wind began to pick up speed, swirling faster and faster until it became a roaring gale.

Finn opened his eyes, and with a shout, he sent the wind crashing forward. It hit the trees with a force that shook the ground, the branches creaking under the pressure. Leaves and debris flew through the air, but Finn kept his focus, controlling the direction and intensity of the wind.

For a moment, he felt like he was the wind, a part of the very element he controlled. It was exhilarating, powerful, but also dangerous. He could feel the raw energy inside him, and he knew that if he wasn't careful, it could spiral out of control.

"Enough!" Leo shouted, stepping forward to ground Finn. "You're pushing too hard!"

Finn snapped back to reality, pulling the wind back with a quick motion. The gale died down almost instantly, leaving the clearing eerily quiet in its wake. Finn dropped to his knees, panting from the effort.

Leo approached, kneeling beside him. "You did great, but you have to pace yourself. Power like that can get away from you if you're not careful."

Finn nodded, wiping the sweat from his brow. "I can feel it how strong it is. But it's like... the more I push, the harder it is to keep control."

"That's why we're here," Maya said, stepping forward. "This is about training, learning how to balance power with control. You're strong, Finn, but we need to make sure you can handle it."

Nora, always calm and focused, added, "You're connected to the wind, but it's still a force of nature. It's unpredictable, wild. The key is learning how to guide it without letting it overwhelm you."

Finn stood up, taking a deep breath. He felt the wind stir around him again, but this time, it was gentler, more in tune with his movements. He nodded, understanding now what he needed to do.

"Let's keep going," he said, determination in his voice. "I need to master this."

The Next Step

Over the next few hours, Finn practiced controlling the wind, learning how to balance power with precision. He discovered that his emotions played a huge role in how the wind responded to him anger made it wild and uncontrollable, while calm focus allowed him to shape it with precision.

By the end of the session, Finn had made remarkable progress. He could create powerful gusts of wind with a simple motion of his hand, but more importantly, he had learned how to control it, how to guide it without letting it get away from him.

As the sun began to set, Finn stood in the clearing, exhausted but satisfied. He had a long way to go, but he was getting closer to mastering his powers.

The others gathered around him, offering words of encouragement. "You're getting stronger, Finn," Sophie said, her eyes filled with admiration. "You're going to be ready for whatever's coming."

Finn smiled, feeling a sense of pride and accomplishment. But he knew that this was only the beginning. There was still so much to learn, and the Darkness was looming closer every day.

"We'll all need to be ready," Finn said, looking at his friends. "This is just the start. We've got a long fight ahead."

Chapter 13

The Training Arena – Light and Shadow

The sun dipped below the horizon, casting long shadows across the forest clearing. As twilight enveloped the training arena, it transformed into a realm of mystery and intrigue, where shadows danced and light flickered. It was the perfect setting for Sophie to explore her newfound abilities.

Finn watched as Sophie stepped into the center of the clearing, her heart racing with both excitement and trepidation. She had always felt an affinity for light, a warmth that enveloped her when she concentrated. But after her recent experiences, she understood that her powers were more complex than she had imagined.

"I'm ready," Sophie declared, her voice steady but laced with nerves.

"Just remember, it's about balance," Leo advised from the edge of the clearing. "Light can be blinding if you're not careful, and shadows can conceal more than just darkness."

Sophie nodded, absorbing the wisdom of her friends. She took a deep breath and focused on the light surrounding her. At first, it flickered softly, like candle flames swaying in the breeze. But as she concentrated, she felt the warmth growing within her, a glowing energy that filled her with confidence.

Sophie extended her arms, palms facing upward, and summoned the light. It responded immediately, brightening and illuminating the clearing. Rays of golden light erupted from her hands, casting away the encroaching shadows and creating a radiant aura around her.

"Beautiful!" Maya exclaimed, her eyes shining with admiration. "You can do this, Sophie!"

With each breath, Sophie harnessed the light, allowing it to swirl and pulse around her. She felt the energy flowing through her, empowering her with a sense of purpose. But as she continued, she remembered Finn's words—balance was essential.

She decided to experiment. With a flick of her wrist, she pulled the light back, creating a stark contrast against the shadows that lingered at the edges of the clearing. The shadows seemed to ripple and shift, almost alive as they danced closer to her.

As she concentrated, Sophie felt a tugging sensation, an urge to explore the darker aspects of her powers. She had always shied away from the shadows, fearing their potential for harm, but now she wanted to understand them.

With a deep breath, Sophie let the shadows intertwine with the light, creating a mesmerizing dance of illumination and darkness. She was in control, guiding the two forces to blend, forming ethereal shapes and patterns in the air.

"Look at that!" Finn said, his voice filled with awe. "You're creating a balance between them!"

Sophie smiled, encouraged by her friends' support. As she continued to weave the light and shadows together, she began to visualize her intent. She imagined the shadows not as a force to be feared but as a tool to enhance her abilities.

But then, as she became more absorbed in her training, a flicker of doubt crept into her mind. What if she lost control? What if the shadows overwhelmed her?

Feeling a rush of anxiety, Sophie instinctively pulled the light back, trying to dispel the shadows. However, the shadows responded with a life of their own, swirling around her, coiling like tendrils.

"Sophie!" Nora shouted, concern etched on her face as she stepped forward.

"Stay calm!" Leo added, his voice steady. "You're in control, Sophie. Remember your training."

Sophie closed her eyes, focusing on her breathing. She recalled Finn's mastery of the wind and how he had learned to harness his emotions. With renewed determination, she opened her eyes and envisioned the light pushing back against the shadows.

The shadows receded, gradually retreating as the light grew stronger. Sophie felt a surge of empowerment as she took charge, mastering the balance between the two forces. With a flick of her wrist, she sent a brilliant burst of light cascading through the clearing, illuminating every corner.

"Wow," Maya whispered, her voice filled with admiration. "You did it!"

Sophie laughed, exhilarated by her success. "I didn't know I could do that! It felt... freeing."

Finn stepped forward, a proud smile on his face. "You've got a real gift, Sophie. But remember, it's not just about power. It's about understanding and using it wisely."

Sophie nodded, feeling a newfound sense of confidence. "I will. Thank you, everyone."

The Next Step

As twilight deepened into night, the group gathered to discuss their training. Each of them had discovered unique strengths, but they understood the importance of supporting one another.

"Next, we should explore our powers together," Nora suggested. "Working as a team will help us learn how to combine our abilities."

"I agree," Finn added. "If we can learn to work in harmony, we'll be much stronger when facing whatever lies ahead."

Sophie felt a surge of excitement. "Let's do it! Together, we can create something incredible."

And with that, the friends decided to embark on a new journey—a journey to discover the potential of their combined powers. The training arena had become their sanctuary, a place where they could grow stronger together, ready to face the challenges that lay ahead.

Chapter 14

The Training Arena – Earth's Embrace

The following day, they returned to the training arena, this time eager to explore Nora's connection to the earth. She had always felt a deep bond with nature, a grounding energy that provided her with strength and wisdom.

As they gathered in the clearing, Finn could feel the anticipation in the air. "Nora, it's your turn! Show us what you can do."

Nora stepped into the center of the clearing, taking a moment to breathe in the earthy scent of the forest. She closed her eyes, allowing herself to connect with the ground beneath her feet. She envisioned the roots of the trees reaching deep into the earth, intertwining with the energy that flowed through it.

"I've always felt a sense of peace when I'm in nature," Nora said, her voice calm and steady. "The earth speaks to me. I can feel its heartbeat."

As she spoke, a gentle breeze rustled the leaves above, and the ground beneath her trembled ever so slightly. She raised her hands, palms down, and closed her eyes, summoning the earth's energy. The ground responded to her call, sending a wave of warmth up through her body.

With a soft chant, Nora began to focus her energy, her hands glowing with a greenish hue. The ground around her began to shift, the soil rising and molding into shapes, forming small mounds and delicate plants that sprouted almost instantly.

"Look at that!" Maya exclaimed, her eyes wide with wonder. "You're bringing the earth to life!"

Nora smiled, feeling the connection deepening. "I can feel the energy of the plants. They're alive, and they respond to me." She continued to manipulate the earth, creating a small garden of flowers and plants in the clearing. Vines twisted and coiled around her fingers, as if welcoming her touch. The air filled with the sweet scent of blossoms, and the colors of the flowers were vibrant, pulsating with life.

But as she worked, Nora began to feel the earth's strength amplifying within her. With every plant she summoned, she felt a surge of power that was both exhilarating and overwhelming.

"Easy there, Nora!" Finn cautioned, sensing the energy building around her. "Remember to stay grounded."

Nora focused, her heart racing as she directed the energy. The ground trembled beneath her feet, and she felt a pull, an instinct to draw upon the raw power of the earth. But instead of a gentle wave, she unleashed a sudden burst, causing the ground to quake violently.

"Mama!" Leo shouted, stumbling back as the earth shifted beneath them.

Nora gasped, realizing her mistake. "I didn't mean to! I just wanted to "

But Finn was quick to intervene. He reached out, channeling the wind to stabilize the area around them. "Nora, focus! Breathe! Remember what we practiced."

Taking a deep breath, Nora closed her eyes and grounded herself again. She felt the roots of the plants beneath her, their strength anchoring her. Slowly, she began to retract the excess energy, allowing the ground to settle back into its peaceful state.

As the tremors subsided, she opened her eyes, panting. "I'm sorry! I got carried away."

"You have incredible power," Maya said, stepping forward. "But it's important to learn how to control it. Just like Finn and Sophie, we all need to find our balance."

Nora nodded, determination gleaming in her eyes. "I'll work on it. I want to be able to protect all of you."

A Journey Together

As the sun began to set, the friends gathered to discuss their progress. Each of them had faced their fears and discovered the depths of their abilities. They knew they still had much to learn, but they were united in their purpose.

"Tomorrow, we should practice combining our powers," Finn suggested, his voice filled with excitement. "If we can work together, we'll be unstoppable."

"I can summon vines to help anchor us while Finn controls the wind," Nora added, her mind racing with possibilities.

"And I can create light to guide us through any darkness," Sophie said, her confidence blossoming.

"We'll figure out how to make our abilities work in harmony," Leo concluded, his eyes bright with enthusiasm. "Together, we can become a force to be reckoned with."

As they left the clearing that night, Finn felt a sense of hope growing within him. They were growing stronger, and with each passing day, they were one step closer to facing the Darkness that loomed ahead.

Chapter 15

The Training Arena – Fire's Heart

The next day, the group returned to the training arena, determined to explore the final aspect of their powers. They gathered in the clearing, ready to tackle the element that had eluded them until now Leo's connection to fire.

"Okay, Leo," Finn said, stepping back to give him space. "It's your time to shine!"

Leo smiled, his eyes gleaming with excitement and a hint of apprehension. "Fire has always been a part of me, but it's also the element that demands respect. I've got to be careful."

He stepped into the center of the clearing, the energy shifting around him. The warmth of the sun beat down, but Leo could feel the coolness of the earth beneath him, a reminder of the balance he needed to maintain.

Taking a deep breath, Leo focused, feeling the heat building within him. He visualized the flames, recalling the times he had played with fire in secret, the exhilaration it brought him. But now, he was ready to harness that energy for a purpose.

With a flick of his wrist, Leo summoned a small flame to dance in his palm, a flickering ember that glowed with life. "See?" he said, grinning at his friends. "This is just the beginning."

But as he spoke, the flame flickered wildly, growing larger and brighter, threatening to engulf him. "Whoa!" he exclaimed, pulling back in surprise.

"Easy, Leo!" Sophie called, concern etching her features. "Control it!"

"I'm trying!" Leo shouted, focusing on the fire, willing it to calm. He remembered Nora's advice about grounding himself and connected with the earth beneath him. With effort, he pulled the fire back, shrinking it down to a manageable size.

"Good job!" Finn encouraged, stepping forward. "Now let's see what you can really do."

Taking a deep breath, Leo focused, allowing the fire to grow once more. This time, he visualized it as a companion an ally rather than a wild beast. With a swift motion, he thrust his hand forward, sending a stream of flames cascading into the air.

The fire danced, swirling in intricate patterns, lighting up the clearing in a warm glow. It was beautiful, mesmerizing, but Leo knew he had to maintain control. He focused, manipulating the flames to create a series of shapes a dragon, a phoenix, and even a small sun.

"Wow!" Nora gasped, her eyes wide with awe. "You're incredible!"

But as Leo continued to push his limits, he felt the heat intensifying. The flames surged, and he could sense the power building within him. It was intoxicating, but he knew he had to rein it in.

"Leo, remember balance!" Maya reminded, her voice filled with urgency. "Don't let the fire consume you!"

With that reminder echoing in his mind, Leo took a step back and concentrated. He envisioned the flames receding, a river of fire flowing back to his palm. Slowly, he retracted the flames, allowing them to shrink until only a small ember remained.

"Phew," he sighed, wiping the sweat from his brow. "That was intense!"

Finn grinned, clapping him on the back. "You did it! You're learning how to control it."

Leo smiled, feeling the exhilaration of success. "Thanks, guys. It's all about finding that balance."

As the sun dipped lower in the sky, the group gathered together, reflecting on their journey. They had each faced their fears, discovered their strengths, and learned the importance of teamwork.

"We've come so far," Sophie said, her voice filled with pride. "But we need to keep practicing together."

"I agree," Finn added. "If we're going to face the Darkness, we have to be ready."

And with that, the friends made a pact a promise to train together, to support one another as they honed their powers. The training arena had become more than just a place for practice; it was their sanctuary, a symbol of their unity.

Chapter 16

The Power of Unity

With their training in full swing, the friends gathered at the training arena each day, eager to explore new ways to combine their powers. They had developed a rhythm, understanding each other's strengths and weaknesses, and learning to trust one another implicitly.

On one particularly bright afternoon, they stood in a circle, ready to practice their combined abilities.

"Let's see what we can create together," Finn suggested, excitement dancing in his eyes. "We've each mastered our individual powers. Now it's time to unite them."

"Sounds good to me!" Leo said, rubbing his hands together. "Let's make something epic!"

Sophie stepped forward, feeling the warmth of the sun on her skin. "I can start with light. I'll create a barrier to protect us while we work."

"Great idea!" Maya chimed in. "I'll use my water to create a mist that can enhance the light."

"I'll call the wind to help spread it evenly," Finn added, his excitement palpable.

"And I'll bring the earth to ground it," Nora finished, feeling the connection to the forest around them.

The Experiment Begins

As they positioned themselves around the clearing, each friend focused on their unique abilities. Sophie raised her hands, summoning the light, creating a shimmering shield that surrounded them. The barrier glowed warmly, casting radiant beams that danced across the trees.

Maya stepped in next, calling forth a gentle stream of water that rose from the ground, forming a thick mist that swirled around them. The light refracted through the mist, creating a dazzling display of colors that filled the clearing.

"I can feel the energy building," Finn said, his voice full of excitement. He extended his arms, summoning the wind. A gentle breeze began to swirl around them, pushing the mist outward and causing it to shimmer even more.

"Perfect!" Nora exclaimed, her eyes shining. She pressed her palms into the earth, sending roots sprouting up around them, anchoring the light and water in place. The combination of elements created a beautiful spectacle, a mesmerizing dance of light, water, wind, and earth.

"Now, let's see how this all works together!" Finn said, a determined look on his face. "On the count of three, we unleash it!"

"Ready!" Sophie called, her heart racing with excitement.

"Let's do this!" Leo added, clenching his fists.

"Three... two... one!" Finn shouted.

A Beautiful Explosion

In a burst of energy, they released their combined powers. The barrier of light flared brilliantly, mingling with the mist to create a stunning, luminous display that shot into the sky. The wind caught the light, sending shimmering particles swirling around them, while the roots anchored it all in place.

The colors blended in a beautiful explosion a dazzling array of hues that illuminated the entire clearing. The air buzzed with energy, and the ground beneath their feet vibrated with the collective force of their powers.

"Look at that!" Maya shouted, her eyes wide with wonder. "It's incredible!"

Finn felt a surge of joy and pride as he watched their powers intertwine. "We did it! We've created something amazing!"

But as the light began to fade, they all felt a strange shift in the air. The colors dimmed, and the warmth of their combined energy dissipated. A sudden chill swept through the clearing, causing Nora to shiver.

"What was that?" she asked, her voice filled with concern.

"I'm not sure," Finn replied, scanning the area. "It felt... different."

"Like something is watching us," Leo added, a frown crossing his face.

Sophie felt a knot forming in her stomach. "We should stay alert. There's something about the Darkness that feels connected to this."

The Gathering Storm

As they gathered themselves, the friends could sense an unease settling in the air. They had played with their powers, but they knew they needed to be cautious.

"Let's keep practicing," Finn suggested, trying to lighten the mood. "We need to be ready for whatever comes our way."

"Agreed," Sophie said, determination shining in her eyes. "We'll train harder, learn more about our powers, and discover how to fight the Darkness."

As the days turned into weeks, their training continued, each friend honing their abilities and deepening their bonds. But they were also becoming more aware of the growing shadows lurking just beyond the forest, a reminder that the Darkness was drawing closer.

Chapter 17

The Heart of Ravenrode

One crisp morning, after a particularly intense training session, the friends gathered to discuss their next steps.

"We've been training for a while now," Finn said, looking around at his friends. "It's time to take the fight to the Darkness."

"But where do we start?" Maya asked, furrowing her brow. "We've learned a lot, but we still don't know enough about what we're facing."

Nora spoke up, her eyes brightening. "What about the legends of the Heart of Ravenrode? I've heard stories about it since we were kids. It's said to be a powerful source of energy that can either protect or unleash destruction."

"I've heard those tales too," Leo added, nodding. "They say the Heart is hidden deep in the forest, guarded by ancient spirits."

"That's it!" Finn exclaimed, feeling a spark of excitement. "If we can find the Heart, we might be able to understand the Darkness better. We could even gain the strength to confront it."

Sophie felt a surge of determination. "Then we should start our journey today. We need to find the Heart and unlock its power before the Darkness consumes Ravenrode."

As they prepared for their journey, each friend packed supplies, knowing they would need everything they had learned along the way. They would face the unknown together, their bond strengthening with every step.

Chapter 18

Into the Forest

With their supplies in tow and their hearts filled with determination, the five friends ventured into the depths of the Ravenrode forest. The familiar trees towered above them, their leaves rustling softly in the breeze.

"Stay close," Finn instructed, leading the way. "We don't know what we might encounter."

As they ventured deeper, the forest began to change. The vibrant greens faded into darker hues, and the air thickened with an unsettling silence. Shadows loomed larger, creeping between the trees as if they were alive.

"This feels... different," Nora whispered, glancing around nervously.

"I can feel it too," Maya replied, her voice low. "It's like the forest is holding its breath."

Finn paused, sensing the tension in the air. "We need to stay vigilant. The Heart is close. I can feel it calling to us."

With each step, the shadows grew more oppressive, but the friends pressed on, drawing strength from one another. Their training had prepared them for challenges, but nothing could fully prepare them for what lay ahead.

The Heart Revealed

After what felt like hours of navigating through the dense forest, they reached a clearing bathed in an otherworldly glow. At the center stood a massive tree, ancient and majestic, its roots sprawling across the ground like a web of magic.

"This must be it," Finn breathed, awe evident in his voice. "The Heart of Ravenrode."

As they approached the tree, they could feel the energy pulsing from it, a rhythm that resonated with their very beings. Sophie reached out, feeling the warmth enveloping her as she laid her palm against the rough bark.

"It's alive," she murmured, her eyes wide. "The Heart is connected to the forest. It holds the balance of light and darkness."

Suddenly, a low rumble echoed through the clearing, causing the ground to tremble beneath their feet. Shadows flickered at the edges of the clearing, and the air grew heavy with an ominous presence.

"We're not alone," Leo said, his voice filled with urgency.

From the shadows emerged figures, cloaked in darkness, their forms shifting and twisting like smoke. They moved closer, their whispers a haunting melody that sent chills down Finn's spine.

"We've come for the Heart," Finn declared, stepping forward, determination in his eyes. "We will protect Ravenrode."

The cloaked figures paused, their eyes glinting with malice. "You cannot control the Heart," one hissed, its voice echoing through the clearing. "It will consume you."

Sophie felt the surge of power from the Heart intensify, resonating with her light. "We won't let it. We'll use its power to fight back."

With a deep breath, the friends joined hands, their bond stronger than ever. They focused on the Heart, channeling their combined energies into a brilliant light that illuminated the clearing, pushing back the encroaching shadows.

A Showdown

The cloaked figures shrieked, their forms writhing as the light expanded. But they were not backing down. "You are fools to challenge us! The Darkness will rise!"

Finn felt the determination of his friends surge within him. "We won't let you take Ravenrode! Together, we are stronger!"

As the light grew, it enveloped the Heart, filling the clearing with warmth and brightness. The shadows writhed and twisted, struggling against the power of their combined abilities.

The friends pushed forward, channeling the energy of the Heart into a powerful wave that surged toward the cloaked figures. With a deafening roar, the shadows recoiled, dissipating into wisps of darkness that faded into the air.

As the last remnants of the shadows vanished, the clearing fell silent. The Heart pulsed gently, its energy now intertwined with the light their powers had created.

"Did we... did we do it?" Maya asked, breathless.

Finn glanced around at his friends, a grin spreading across his face. "We did! We stood together and faced the Darkness!"

But Sophie felt a weight in her chest, a lingering sense of unease. "This isn't over. The Darkness will return, and we need to be ready."

With that realization hanging in the air, the friends made a pact to protect Ravenrode, to stand united against the threats that loomed ahead. They had discovered their powers, learned to work together, and faced the shadows that threatened their home.

Chapter 19

The Return of Shadows

With the Heart of Ravenrode still pulsing with the energy of their victory, the five friends left the clearing, a sense of accomplishment warming their hearts. But as they emerged from the depths of the forest, the feeling of unease settled back in. They knew their battle was far from over.

The journey back to their village felt heavier. The trees, once vibrant and full of life, seemed to whisper secrets of an approaching storm. Finn led the way, his senses heightened, each rustle in the underbrush setting his heart racing.

"We need to strengthen our defenses," Leo said, breaking the silence. "The Darkness may have retreated for now, but it won't stay away for long."

Sophie nodded, her brow furrowed. "I've been thinking about the ancient book. It mentioned ways to strengthen the Heart and protect Ravenrode. We need to decipher its secrets before it's too late."

"Agreed," Nora said, her voice steady. "But we can't do it alone. We should enlist the help of the Elders. They might have insights into the book and its connection to the Heart."

As they made their way back to the village, the friends discussed strategies for gathering information. Each step felt like a ticking clock, a reminder that they were running out of time.

Chapter 20

Secrets of the Elders

The following day, the friends approached the village's Elder council. They were greeted with curious looks, the Elders exchanging whispers as they entered the dimly lit hall. The air was thick with anticipation, and Finn could feel the weight of their elders' gaze.

Elder Rowan, the oldest among them, motioned for silence. "You seek our wisdom, young ones. What troubles you?"

Finn stepped forward, determination in his eyes. "We've encountered dark forces threatening Ravenrode. We discovered the Heart of Ravenrode and fought off shadows, but we believe they will return. We need to know more about the ancient magic and how we can protect our home."

The Elders shared knowing glances, and Finn could sense the tension in the room. Elder Rowan leaned forward, his voice grave. "You have done well to confront the Darkness. But the Heart is not simply a source of power. It is a beacon, attracting both light and shadow. You must tread carefully."

"Is there a way to strengthen its defenses?" Nora asked, her voice steady. "The ancient book we found may hold the key, but we need guidance."

Elder Rowan nodded, his expression thoughtful. "The book contains ancient knowledge that many have forgotten. It speaks of rituals to reinforce the Heart's magic, but it also warns of a great sacrifice. The balance of power requires more than simple spells."

"What kind of sacrifice?" Sophie asked, her heart racing.

"It varies," Elder Rowan replied. "Sometimes it is the power within oneself, other times it is a bond an act of true unity. To strengthen the Heart, you must be willing to give a piece of yourselves."

Finn exchanged glances with his friends, a mix of fear and determination swirling within him. They had already faced so much together, but the idea of sacrifice sent a chill down his spine.

"We'll do whatever it takes," Finn vowed, his voice steady. "We need to protect Ravenrode and each other."

The Elders nodded solemnly. "Very well. We will guide you in the rituals, but know that the path ahead will test your strength and resolve."

Chapter 21

The First Ritual

Back in the training arena, the friends gathered to discuss their next steps. The Elders had provided them with a series of rituals, each designed to strengthen the Heart and their connection to it.

"According to the Elders," Maya explained, her eyes wide with excitement, "the first ritual involves harnessing our individual powers and creating a protective barrier around the Heart."

"Let's get started," Finn said, feeling the urgency of their mission. "We need to perform this ritual before the shadows return."

They gathered at the clearing, each friend preparing to channel their powers. "Remember," Sophie reminded them, "we need to focus on our bond and trust in each other. This ritual won't work if we're not united."

With that, they began the ritual. Sophie stood at the center, her light illuminating the clearing. Finn called upon the wind, swirling it around them, while Maya summoned water from a nearby stream, creating a protective barrier. Leo called forth the earth, anchoring their powers, and Nora connected with the forest, allowing its ancient wisdom to flow through them.

As their energies converged, the air crackled with magic, a radiant barrier forming around the Heart.

"I can feel it working!" Leo exclaimed, excitement bubbling in his voice.

But just as they reached the peak of their power, the shadows flickered at the edges of the clearing, dark tendrils creeping closer.

"Stay strong!" Finn shouted, the wind howling around them. "We can't let them through!"

Chapter 22

A Battle of Light and Shadow

The shadows surged forward, dark figures emerging from the trees, determined to breach their defenses.

"We have to hold them back!" Nora cried, her voice filled with urgency.

Finn focused, channeling the wind into a protective barrier. "Keep the light strong, Sophie!"

Sophie concentrated harder, her light expanding outward. The shadows recoiled, hissing in frustration, but they didn't retreat.

"We need to combine our powers!" Maya urged. "If we strengthen the barrier, we can push them away!"

With a deep breath, they worked together, channeling their energy into a single point. The light surged, and the barrier glowed brighter, pushing back the encroaching darkness.

The shadows writhed, but the barrier held strong.

Suddenly, one of the dark figures lunged forward, its twisted form breaking through the barrier. Finn's heart raced as he faced it, instinctively calling forth the wind to push it back.

"Everyone, focus!" Finn shouted. "We have to work together!"

With a surge of energy, they combined their powers once more, and the light exploded outward, scattering the shadows like smoke in the wind.

But as the last shadow faded, they knew this wasn't the end. The battle had only just begun.

Chapter 23

The Darkest Hour

Exhausted but resolute, the friends gathered together in the clearing, breaths coming in heavy gasps after their intense battle with the shadows. The air was thick with the remnants of magic, crackling around them as they processed what had just happened.

Finn stood at the forefront, surveying his friends each one a pillar of strength in the wake of chaos. Sophie's light flickered faintly, the strain of maintaining it evident on her face. Maya leaned against a tree, her hands trembling slightly. Leo's brow glistened with sweat, and Nora was still catching her breath, her eyes wide with the adrenaline of battle.

"We held them back," Finn finally said, breaking the heavy silence. "But this is just the beginning. We can't let our guard down."

Sophie nodded, her expression solemn. "The Darkness won't stop. It's searching for a way to breach our defenses. We need to understand why it's targeting us, and what it wants from the Heart."

"What do you think it wants?" Maya asked.

Finn glanced around, contemplating their situation. "The Heart is more than just a source of power; it's a connection to Ravenrode itself. Maybe the Darkness wants to disrupt that connection."

"That would explain why it attacked us," Leo said. "If it can weaken the Heart, it could gain control over Ravenrode."

Nora looked toward the horizon, where the sun was setting. "We can't let that happen. We have to protect the Heart and each other. We need to be united."

Finn felt the weight of her words settle in his chest. "You're right. But we need to prepare. We have to train harder and dig deeper into our powers."

Sophie nodded, a flicker of hope igniting in her eyes. "The Elders said there are rituals and spells that can strengthen our connection to the Heart. We need to focus on those."

Finn felt a sense of unity forming among them. "Let's make a plan. We'll divide our time between training and studying the book."

Maya stepped forward. "And we can set up a training schedule! Each of us can focus on our strengths and work together to enhance our weaknesses."

As they discussed their plans, Finn felt a sense of purpose grow within him. They had to be ready, not just for themselves, but for all of Ravenrode.

A Gathering Storm

As twilight descended over Ravenrode, the friends gathered in their makeshift training arena. Finn stood at the center, heart racing with anticipation.

"Okay, let's start with our individual powers," he said. "We'll alternate between practicing our strengths and working on our weaknesses."

Sophie stepped forward first, summoning her light. It glowed brilliantly, illuminating the clearing. "I want to work on maintaining my light longer," she said.

Maya joined in, ready to help. "I can create a water mist to amplify Sophie's light."

"Let's do it," Finn said, excitement bubbling in his chest. As they combined their powers, the light radiated brilliantly, casting away the darkness.

But as they reveled in their success, Finn felt a flicker of doubt. Would this be enough when the Darkness returned?

A Moment of Reflection

As the night deepened, they paused to catch their breath. The clearing was peaceful, bathed in the soft glow of their combined magic.

"Today was a good start," Finn said. "But we need to push ourselves harder."

Sophie looked thoughtful. "The book mentions different kinds of shadows. If we can understand the Darkness we face, we might find weaknesses."

"Exactly," Leo agreed. "Each shadow could have a different origin. We can't assume they're all the same."

As they discussed their plans, Finn felt the weight of their task but also the warmth of their friendship. Together, they were more than just a group of friends; they were a team, bound by their shared purpose.

The Journey Ahead

With their training and plans set, the friends began to forge a new path one filled with uncertainty but also with hope. The following days would be filled with study, training, and preparations.

But beneath the surface of their efforts, an ominous storm loomed. The Darkness would return, more powerful than before, and it would stop at nothing to achieve its goals.

Finn felt the stirrings of a challenge awaiting them, a battle that would test the limits of their powers and their friendship.

Chapter 24

Trials of Power

The forest clearing hummed with anticipation as the five friends prepared to push their abilities further than ever before. Finn stood at the center, his gaze steady as he surveyed his companions.

"Today's about control," Finn began, addressing the group. "We've all felt our powers growing, but power without control is dangerous. We need to master what we have."

The others nodded in agreement, their expressions serious.

Sophie's Light

Sophie stepped forward first. Her ability to summon light had always been a beacon for the group, but she knew there was more she needed to do. Taking a deep breath, Sophie summoned her power. The warm glow radiated from her palms, expanding until it formed a dome of pure light around the group.

The shield was beautiful, but as the seconds passed, Sophie's concentration wavered. The light flickered, and cracks appeared in the dome.

"Hold it!" Finn urged, his voice steady but encouraging.

Sophie closed her eyes, focusing every ounce of energy she had into maintaining the light. Gradually, the cracks disappeared, and the dome became solid once again. She held it for a moment longer before letting it dissolve, collapsing to the ground with exhaustion.

"You did it," Finn said softly, helping her to her feet.

"I need to get stronger," Sophie replied, panting. "This was just a taste."

Leo's Fire

Next was Leo. His powers over fire had always been impressive, but volatile. He stepped forward, taking a deep breath, and summoned flames that flickered to life in his hands. The fire began as a gentle glow, but quickly grew into a roaring blaze, casting an orange light across the training arena.

"Keep it contained," Finn instructed, watching as Leo struggled to hold the flames back.

Leo clenched his fists, the fire swirling around him, nearly out of control. The heat intensified, causing the air to shimmer and crackle, while sparks leaped into the air, threatening to spread beyond his control.

Just as the fire seemed on the verge of breaking free, Leo pulled it back, the flames settling into a steady flame that danced in his palms. He let out a sigh of relief as the blaze calmed, leaving only the warm glow.

"I've got a lot of work to do," Leo muttered, wiping sweat from his brow.

"You're getting there," Finn said. "We'll keep working on balance."

Chapter 25

Shadows and Earth

The clearing in the woods felt heavy with anticipation as the friends stood in a circle, each bracing for their next trial. The wind whispered through the trees, rustling the leaves, but even the air seemed to be holding its breath, as if the forest itself sensed the gravity of what was to come.

Nora stepped forward, her expression determined but guarded. The shadows that lingered at the edges of the clearing responded to her presence, like old friends waiting to be called upon. Her power over shadows had always been mysterious even to her and today, she would push those boundaries in ways none of them had seen before.

Nora's Shadows

She raised her hands, and the darkness obeyed. Slowly, the shadows slithered across the ground, coiling at her feet before rising like a living entity. With a deep breath, Nora began to shape them, her focus intense as she willed the shadows into a swirling vortex.

The shadows spun, forming a dark, swirling portal before her. For a moment, everything seemed under control, and Nora felt a sense of accomplishment. But then, something changed. The shadows rippled, as if something from the other side was pressing against them. Her heart skipped a beat as the portal trembled.

Suddenly, a deep whisper echoed from the darkness a voice, not her own, trying to reach her.

"Nora, close it!" Finn's urgent voice cut through her concentration, sensing the danger.

Nora's breath quickened, her control faltering. With a swift motion, she slammed her hands down, closing the portal just as the shadows threatened to break free. The swirling mass dissipated into the earth, leaving the clearing eerily still.

She staggered back, breath ragged, eyes wide. "There's something... beyond the shadows," she whispered, her voice trembling. "Something alive."

"We'll figure it out," Finn assured her, stepping forward. "You did great, but we need to understand what you're tapping into."

Nora nodded, but her thoughts were still consumed by the voice that had whispered her name.

Maya's Elements

It was Maya's turn now. She stepped into the circle, her connection to the earth and water always a source of calm and strength for the group. But today, she was going to try something new. Her powers had evolved, and with the rising dangers, she needed to push her abilities further.

Maya knelt, placing her hands on the earth. She called to the nearby stream, and water surged toward her, spiraling up into the air. At the same time, the ground beneath her feet began to shift, rising to form a mound of earth. With a deep breath, Maya commanded the two elements water and earth to merge.

The air around her shimmered as the two forces intertwined, forming a living sculpture of mud that hung suspended in midair. For a moment, the solid-liquid creation held, swirling like a piece of art made from the very essence of nature.

But as Maya pushed further, trying to shape the mud into something more, her control slipped. The delicate balance between water and earth faltered, and the swirling mass collapsed, splattering at her feet.

"I was so close," Maya muttered, her frustration evident as she shook her head.

"You're getting there," Finn reassured her, offering a smile. "It's about timing and precision. We'll keep practicing."

A United Front

As the day wore on, the friends continued their trials, each facing their own challenges. The weight of their growing powers was palpable, but so was the tension. Ravenrode's mysteries were becoming more complex, and the darkness that lingered just beyond their reach was no longer a distant threat.

Sophie, Leo, Finn, Maya, and Nora stood together, tired but resolute. They had each felt the strain of pushing their abilities further than ever before, and yet, something had shifted within the group. Their bond was growing stronger, a force that went beyond their individual powers.

"This is just the beginning," Finn said, his voice steady but filled with determination. "We're stronger together, and we're only going to get better."

Nora glanced at the shadows, still wary of what they had shown her, and Maya looked down at the pool of mud at her feet, knowing she was on the verge of something powerful. Together, they were no longer the same children who had been swept into the world of magic. They were becoming something more something powerful.

As they stood there in the fading light of the day, they knew one thing for certain: the road ahead was filled with danger, but they would face it united, whatever came next.

Chapter 26

The Call of the Unknown

The night after their trials was unusually quiet in Ravenrode. The small village, nestled in the shadows of towering trees, seemed to hold its breath as if anticipating the next move. The five friends sat together in Finn's family home, their minds still buzzing with the intensity of their training. They had begun to understand the depth of their powers, but the mystery surrounding them was growing darker, more urgent.

Sophie paced back and forth, unable to sit still. "There's something we're missing," she muttered, running her fingers through her hair. "Something that's been right in front of us this whole time."

"Like what?" Leo asked, leaning back in his chair, arms crossed. His fire powers still left a faint warmth around him, but it was his usual cocky confidence that seemed to have dimmed after the day's trial.

Nora, sitting near the window where the shadows clung like silent sentinels, spoke quietly. "It's not just about our powers. The magic in Ravenrode... it's tied to something ancient. We're being drawn toward it."

Maya nodded, her calm composure steady as always. "I felt it too. The earth responds, but it's like something beneath the surface is waiting. Watching."

Finn, who had been quiet, finally spoke. "The trials are preparing us for something bigger. But we need to find out what. We need to go deeper into the forest, to where it all began the Heart of Ravenrode."

The room fell silent. The Heart of Ravenrode was a place shrouded in legend. Even as children, they had heard whispers about it. A place where the magic of the land was strongest, where the ancient forces that governed the forest were said to be sleeping.

"I've been sensing it for a while now," Sophie said. "The magic in the Heart is waking up, and it's pulling us toward it."

Nora's eyes darkened. "But not just us. Something else is moving too. The shadows... they're stirring."

The others exchanged uneasy glances.

"What do you mean?" Maya asked.

Nora hesitated, remembering the voice she had heard during her trial with the shadows. "There's something beyond the shadows. Something powerful. And it's waiting for us to make the first move."

Into the Depths of Ravenrode

The following morning, the five friends gathered at the edge of the village, standing before the ancient forest that had always been their home, yet somehow now felt foreign and dangerous. The trees loomed like silent giants, their branches swaying gently in the wind as if whispering secrets they weren't ready to hear.

"We need to be careful," Finn said, tightening his grip on his staff. "We're not just wandering into the woods anymore. This is a journey into the unknown."

Leo smirked, though his eyes showed traces of nerves. "I say bring it on. Whatever's out there, we can handle it."

Sophie cast him a warning look. "Let's not get overconfident. We don't know what we'll find."

With that, they stepped into the forest. The path they took was one they had traveled many times, but today, it felt different. The further they ventured, the more the air seemed to thicken with magic. It wasn't just in the trees or the earth it was in the very atmosphere, a heavy, humming presence that set their nerves on edge.

As they walked, Maya occasionally touched the ground, feeling the pulse of the earth beneath her. "The magic is stronger here," she said quietly. "Almost as if the forest itself is alive."

"It is alive," Nora said, her voice low. "And it's watching us."

The First Sign

After hours of trekking through the thick underbrush, they came upon something none of them had expected: an ancient stone circle. The stones, weathered by time, stood tall and imposing, each one marked with strange symbols that none of them recognized.

"What is this?" Sophie asked, stepping forward to examine one of the stones. She traced her fingers over the markings, feeling a faint energy pulse beneath her fingertips.

"It's a ward," Nora said suddenly, her eyes narrowing. "A protective circle. Someone put this here a long time ago to keep something out... or keep something in."

Finn frowned. "Do you think it's connected to the Heart?"

"Definitely," Maya said, her eyes scanning the circle. "This magic is old, older than anything we've ever dealt with."

As they stood within the circle, a sudden gust of wind blew through the clearing, causing the trees to sway violently. The ground trembled beneath their feet, and for a moment, it felt as though the entire forest was shifting around them.

"Something's happening," Leo muttered, flames sparking in his hands instinctively. "Get ready."

A Shift in the Magic

Suddenly, the symbols on the stones began to glow, a soft, eerie light that pulsed in time with the heartbeat of the forest. The magic they had felt all around them seemed to converge in the center of the circle, forming a swirling vortex of energy.

"We need to leave," Finn said urgently. "This isn't safe."

But before they could move, the ground beneath them cracked open, and a dark mist began to seep up from the earth. The mist coiled and twisted, forming a shape a figure made entirely of shadows. Nora's breath caught in her throat. "It's them," she whispered. "The shadows."

The figure loomed before them, its form shifting and writhing as if it were alive. It had no face, no features, but its presence was overwhelming. It was like looking into the void into something that wasn't meant to be seen.

"What... is that?" Leo asked, his voice shaking slightly.

The figure spoke, its voice a low, rumbling whisper that seemed to come from everywhere and nowhere at once. "You have come to the Heart. But you are not ready. The forces that govern this place will test you. Only those who understand the balance of power may proceed."

The mist swirled faster, and the figure's shape began to solidify. "Prepare yourselves," it said, its voice growing louder. "The trials of Ravenrode have only just begun."

The Beginning of the Trials

As the figure dissolved back into the mist, the friends exchanged uneasy glances. They had faced trials before, but this was different. The magic of Ravenrode itself was preparing to test them and this time, it wasn't just about mastering their powers. It was about understanding the very forces that governed the world they lived in.

"We can do this," Finn said, his voice steady. "We've trained for this."

Maya nodded, her resolve strengthening. "We have to find the Heart. Whatever is waiting for us, we'll face it together."

With a final glance at the glowing stones, they stepped deeper into the forest, ready to face whatever challenges lay ahead. The Heart of Ravenrode was calling to them, and they would not turn back now.

Chapter 27

Into the Heart of Ravenrode

The forest seemed to close in around them, the air thick with an unspoken tension as they ventured deeper toward the Heart of Ravenrode. Each step felt like a journey into the unknown, the familiar paths of the woods now twisted and unfamiliar, as if the land itself was shifting in response to their presence.

Finn took the lead, his heart pounding in his chest. He could feel the magic in the air, humming beneath his skin, urging him forward. "Stay close," he whispered, his voice barely louder than the rustling leaves. "We don't know what we're walking into."

Nora, who had been silent for much of the journey, moved like a shadow at the edge of the group. Her senses were heightened, attuned to the darkness that seemed to ripple just beyond the trees. "There's something out there," she said softly, her voice laced with caution. "Watching us."

The others exchanged glances, their nerves on edge. Whatever lay ahead, it wasn't going to let them pass without a fight.

The Silent Watcher

The path before them narrowed, winding through thick trees whose branches tangled above, blocking out most of the light. It was as if the forest had grown darker, more oppressive, the deeper they went. Finn could hear his own breathing, steady but filled with the tension of what might be lurking ahead.

Suddenly, Sophie stopped, her eyes wide. "Did you hear that?" she whispered, her voice trembling.

Maya looked around, her hand instinctively reaching for the water that bubbled from a nearby spring. "What is it?"

There was no sound. The forest had fallen completely silent, as though holding its breath, waiting for something to happen.

"It's too quiet," Leo muttered, the usual fire in his voice dimmed by the eerie stillness. He held out his hand, a small flame flickering to life in his palm, casting faint shadows that danced along the ground.

As they stood frozen, a low growl echoed through the trees, sending a chill down their spines. Finn's eyes darted toward the sound, his grip tightening on his staff. "Whatever it is, it's close."

Without warning, a dark shape emerged from the shadows. It moved with unnatural speed, darting between the trees, its form flickering as if it were made of the very darkness that surrounded them.

Nora reacted first, her shadow magic flaring to life. "Stay back!" she shouted, raising her hand as tendrils of darkness shot from her fingertips, trying to entrap the creature.

But the shape was too fast. It slipped through her shadows, its eyes gleaming as it circled them, watching, waiting.

The Guardian's Challenge

Before Finn could call for action, the creature lunged, faster than any of them could react. Finn barely had time to summon the wind, pushing the others out of its path. The creature's form was fluid, shifting and warping like smoke, but its presence was undeniable a force of malevolence that radiated from it like a palpable weight.

It wasn't just a beast it was a Guardian, bound to the Heart of Ravenrode, testing those who dared come too close.

"We have to stop it!" Leo shouted, flames roaring to life in his hands as he unleashed a torrent of fire toward the creature.

The fire hit the Guardian, but it barely flinched, the flames seeming to pass through its form as though it were made of smoke. It turned toward Leo, its eyes gleaming with a dark, ancient intelligence.

Maya stepped forward, her voice steady despite the fear gripping her. "We need to use more than just force! It's tied to the forest, to the magic here."

"Then what do we do?" Leo asked, his flames faltering.

Sophie's mind raced. "The stones!" she cried suddenly. "The symbols! They're a part of the magic that controls this place. If we can tap into it, we can weaken the Guardian."

Nora's eyes darkened as realization struck. "We have to understand the balance of power here. It's not just about fighting it's about control."

The Ancient Symbols

The Guardian circled them again, growing more aggressive with every moment, but Sophie was already moving, her eyes scanning the trees. "Look!" she pointed. Along the bark of the nearest tree, glowing faintly, were the same ancient symbols they had seen in the stone circle.

"It's a binding spell," Sophie murmured, her fingers tracing the symbols. "The magic here is meant to control the Guardian."

Maya, quick to catch on, stepped up beside her. "If we can strengthen it, we might be able to trap it."

"But how?" Finn asked, barely dodging another strike from the Guardian as it lunged toward him. "We don't have time!"

Sophie turned to Finn, her eyes blazing with determination. "We need to combine our powers earth, wind, fire, water, shadow all of it. The forest responds to all of us."

Nora nodded, already drawing the shadows to her, her hands steady. "We can do this."

A Battle of Balance

As the Guardian closed in, the five friends moved into position, standing in a circle around the glowing symbols. The ground beneath them trembled, the power of the forest responding to their combined presence.

"Now!" Finn shouted.

Maya slammed her hands into the earth, vines erupting from the ground, wrapping around the Guardian's shifting form. Leo followed, sending streams of fire along the vines, strengthening their grip. Nora wove her shadows through the flames, binding the Guardian with a darkness that matched its own.

Sophie closed her eyes, her mind reaching out to the ancient magic that pulsed through the forest. "We need more," she whispered, her voice barely audible. "Finn, the wind."

Finn nodded, his heart racing as he called the wind, channeling it through the trees, guiding the magic toward the Guardian. The wind howled, swirling around them, carrying the energy of the forest itself.

The Guardian screeched, its form flickering, weakening under the combined force of their magic. The ancient symbols on the trees flared to life, glowing brighter and brighter as the Guardian struggled against the bonds that held it.

"We've almost got it!" Maya shouted, her face contorted with the effort of holding the magic in place.

The Guardian roared one last time before it collapsed, its form dissolving into the ground, leaving nothing but a faint mist in its wake.

The Heart Awaits

For a moment, none of them spoke. The forest was still again, the air heavy with the lingering magic of their battle.

"We did it," Leo said finally, his voice filled with both relief and disbelief.

Nora glanced at the spot where the Guardian had fallen. "That was just the beginning," she murmured. "The Heart of Ravenrode is still waiting for us."

Sophie nodded, her eyes distant. "And it's not going to let us pass without a final test."

Finn tightened his grip on his staff. "Then we face whatever comes next. Together."

With renewed determination, they moved deeper into the forest, the path ahead now darker than before. The Heart of Ravenrode was close, its ancient power pulsing beneath the earth, calling to them. They were ready for the final trial ready to face the truth that had been hidden in the shadows all along.

Chapter 28

The Heart's Whisper

The clearing before them was a place of ancient power. The towering obelisk at its center pulsed faintly, its carvings glowing in soft, rhythmic waves. But the magic in the air wasn't comforting it was unsettling, as if the Heart of Ravenrode was alive, watching them, waiting for them to make a move.

Finn took a step forward, his eyes fixed on the obelisk. "We've come this far," he said, more to himself than to the others. "We need to understand what this place really is."

The others gathered around him, their eyes wary but curious. The air was thick with tension, as though the very trees around them held secrets they weren't ready to share.

Sophie reached out hesitantly, her fingers barely grazing the surface of the stone. The energy that coursed through it sent a shiver down her spine. "There's something about this magic," she murmured. "It's old... too old. And it's not just elemental."

Nora, standing close to the shadows that danced at the edge of the clearing, narrowed her eyes. "I can feel it too. There's darkness here, but it's hiding. Waiting for the right moment."

Maya knelt beside Sophie, placing her hands on the ground. The earth beneath her fingers hummed with energy, a deep, ancient pulse that seemed to come from the very roots of the forest. "The Heart is connected to everything in Ravenrode," she said. "The earth, the water, even the shadows."

Leo stood back, his flames flickering at his fingertips as he observed the scene. "So what now? Do we wake it up and see what happens?"

Finn shook his head. "No, not yet. We don't know what we're dealing with."

A Silent Warning

The moment Finn spoke, the obelisk's glow intensified, sending a ripple of energy through the clearing. It was subtle, but enough to make the ground tremble beneath their feet. Sophie drew back, her eyes wide with alarm.

"Did you feel that?" she asked, her voice barely above a whisper.

Before anyone could answer, the wind shifted. It wasn't a natural breeze; it was sharp, cold, and filled with the distant sound of whispers. Finn felt the hair on the back of his neck rise as the voices in the wind grew louder, though the words were indistinct, like fragments of a forgotten language.

"They're talking to us," Nora said, her voice low and calm. She closed her eyes, letting the shadows at her feet curl around her ankles. "I can almost hear them."

Leo looked around, his fiery confidence flickering. "What are they saying?"

Sophie's brow furrowed. "It's not clear. But it feels like a warning." Maya stood abruptly, her connection to the earth humming with urgency. "We're not alone here."

As if on cue, the ground beneath the obelisk cracked slightly, releasing a thin tendril of dark mist. The mist spiraled upward, twisting and coiling like a serpent. It wasn't aggressive, but its presence was unnerving.

"What is that?" Leo asked, his flames burning brighter as he prepared for whatever might come next.

Nora's voice was steady, though her eyes were fixed on the mist. "It's part of the Heart's magic. But it's not here to help us."

The Enigma of the Obelisk

The mist circled the obelisk, intertwining with the glowing symbols carved into the stone. It was as if the obelisk itself was responding to the dark energy, feeding off it. Sophie stepped closer, her curiosity battling the fear that tugged at the edges of her mind.

"The symbols," she murmured. "They're changing."

Finn followed her gaze, watching as the ancient carvings shifted before his eyes, the lines rearranging themselves into new patterns. It was as if the obelisk was alive, adapting to their presence.

"We need to figure out what this means," Maya said, her voice tense. "The Heart is trying to tell us something, but we don't have all the pieces."

Finn's mind raced. They had encountered powerful magic before, but this felt different deeper. It was as though the Heart of Ravenrode wasn't just a source of power, but a living entity with its own will, its own purpose.

Sophie traced the newly formed symbols with her fingers, her eyes narrowing in concentration. "These are wards. Old ones. They're meant to contain something."

Leo's flames flickered out for a moment as he stepped forward. "Contain what?"

"I don't know," Sophie admitted. "But whatever it is, it's connected to the darkness we've been sensing."

Nora crossed her arms, her shadows flickering in and out of the corners of her vision. "It's more than just darkness. There's something... ancient here. Something older than the forest itself."

Finn's grip on his staff tightened. "We're not ready to face it yet. We need more answers."

Whispers in the Dark

The obelisk trembled again, and this time, the whispers grew louder. They were closer now, clearer, though still indistinct. The voices seemed to come from all directions, wrapping around the group like a shroud.

"What are they saying?" Leo asked, his voice filled with frustration. "I can't make any sense of it."

Nora closed her eyes, focusing on the sound. Her connection to the shadows made her more attuned to the whispers, but even she struggled to decipher them. "They're speaking in riddles," she said slowly. "But I can feel their intent. They want something from us."

Sophie shivered. "It's like they're testing us. Seeing if we're worthy."

"Worthy of what?" Maya asked, her voice tight.

Before anyone could answer, the ground beneath them shifted. The crack at the base of the obelisk widened, and the dark mist began to pour out in greater quantities. It moved faster now, swirling around the group in a tight circle, as if trapping them in place.

"We need to move!" Finn shouted, summoning a gust of wind to push the mist away. But the wind barely made a dent in the dark magic that surrounded them.

Nora's shadows flared to life, trying to contain the mist, but it was too strong. The darkness pushed back against her control, slipping through her grasp like water through a sieve.

"It's no use," she said through gritted teeth. "This magic is too old, too powerful."

A Deeper Mystery

Just when they thought they were trapped, the mist suddenly pulled back, retreating to the base of the obelisk. The clearing fell silent once more, but the tension in the air remained.

"That was just a warning," Sophie said, her voice shaky. "The Heart is testing us, seeing how far we're willing to go."

Finn looked around, his heart still racing. "We need to leave. We're not ready for this."

But as they turned to go, the ground beneath them rumbled, and a voice deep, ancient, and filled with authority spoke from the obelisk.

"You have been chosen," the voice said, its words echoing in the air around them. "The Heart of Ravenrode waits

for you. But only those who understand its true power may proceed."

The group froze, staring at the obelisk in stunned silence. The voice wasn't like the whispers they had heard before it was clear, commanding, and unmistakably tied to the magic of the Heart.

"What does it mean?" Maya asked, her voice filled with uncertainty.

"I think we've only scratched the surface," Sophie replied, her eyes fixed on the obelisk. "There's more to this than we ever realized."

Nora's voice was steady, though her eyes gleamed with determination. "We have to uncover the truth. Whatever the Heart is hiding, we need to find it before the darkness does."

Finn nodded, his resolve hardening. "Then we keep going. No turning back now."

As they stepped deeper into the clearing, the obelisk's glow intensified, casting long shadows across the ground. The Heart of Ravenrode was waiting for them, but the mystery of its true purpose was far from being solved.

And they had a feeling the final test was still to come.

Chapter 29

Echoes of the Heart

The glow of the obelisk lingered in the air, casting eerie shadows across the clearing as the friends stood at its base, trying to process the weight of the voice that had spoken. Each of them felt it deep in their bones a call, a challenge, and a warning, all rolled into one. The Heart of Ravenrode wasn't merely waiting for them to unlock its secrets; it was watching, and it had plans of its own.

Sophie pressed her palm against the stone, feeling the ancient energy pulsating beneath the surface. "It feels like it's alive," she whispered, her voice barely audible. "Like it's waiting for something something from us."

Leo took a step forward, his flames dancing at his fingertips. "I don't like this. It's like a trap, and we're walking straight into it."

Maya placed a hand on his shoulder, her calm presence steadying the group. "It's not a trap," she said softly, her voice filled with quiet conviction. "But it is testing us. The Heart is ancient it's seen things we can't even imagine. And it's not going to let us pass unless we prove ourselves."

Nora stood a little apart from the group, her eyes narrowed as she watched the shadows shifting in the corners of the clearing. The darkness felt more oppressive here, more alive, as if the shadows themselves were whispering secrets. "There's more to this than we're seeing," she murmured, her voice low and guarded. "The shadows are restless. Whatever the Heart is hiding, it doesn't want us to leave until we uncover it."

Finn, who had been silent up until now, looked around at his friends. He could feel the weight of the magic in the air, heavy and thick like a storm on the horizon. "We're not turning back," he said firmly. "We came here for answers, and we're going to find them."

A Sudden Shift

As Finn spoke, the ground beneath their feet trembled again. This time, it wasn't just a minor tremor the earth itself seemed to shudder, as though something deep beneath the surface had awakened.

Maya knelt quickly, pressing her hands to the ground. "There's something moving," she said, her eyes wide with alarm. "Something big."

Before anyone could react, the obelisk's glow intensified, and the air around them crackled with energy. The carvings on the stone began to shift again, rearranging themselves into new symbols, patterns that pulsed with power.

Sophie took a step back, her heart racing. "It's changing."

Leo raised his hands, fire flaring up in defense. "I'm ready for whatever this thing is about to throw at us."

But before Leo could unleash his flames, the ground erupted in a shower of dirt and stone. From the depths of the earth, a massive shape emerged an ancient stone creature, covered in moss and vines, its eyes glowing with the same eerie light as the obelisk. It stood at least ten feet tall, towering over them with an air of ancient authority.

"What... is that?" Leo muttered, his voice filled with awe.

Maya took a sharp breath. "It's a Guardian," she said, her voice barely above a whisper. "But it's not like the others. This one's older much older."

Nora stepped forward, her shadows swirling around her. "It's tied to the Heart," she said, her voice calm despite the tension in the air. "We have to understand what it wants."

The Guardian's Challenge

The creature didn't attack immediately. Instead, it stood there, watching them with glowing eyes, as if waiting for them to make the first move. Its presence was overwhelming, a force of nature that felt as old as Ravenrode itself.

Finn raised his staff, summoning the wind to stir around him. "We need to be ready," he said, his eyes locked on the Guardian. "It's not just here to watch us."

The Guardian's eyes flashed, and suddenly, the ground beneath their feet cracked open, sending a wave of energy surging through the clearing. Maya reacted instinctively, summoning vines from the earth to wrap around the creature's legs, trying to hold it in place.

But the Guardian was strong. It tore through the vines with ease, its movements slow but deliberate. It wasn't just attacking it was testing them.

"We can't just fight it like the others," Sophie called out, her mind racing as she tried to make sense of the symbols on the obelisk. "It's tied to the magic here. We need to understand how to beat it, not just overpower it."

Leo, his flames burning brighter than ever, stepped forward. "Then what do we do? We can't just stand here and wait for it to crush us."

Nora's eyes flickered as the shadows around her grew darker, coiling like serpents. "I can feel its connection to the Heart," she said, her voice calm but tense. "It's not just a guardian it's a gatekeeper. If we want to get past it, we need to solve the riddle of the Heart."

The Puzzle of the Heart

Sophie's eyes lit up as she understood what Nora meant. "The symbols!" she shouted, pointing to the obelisk. "They're not just wards they're instructions. The Heart is giving us a puzzle to solve."

Finn glanced at the obelisk, then back at the Guardian, which was still moving toward them, though slower now. "A puzzle? What kind of puzzle?"

Sophie moved quickly, her hands tracing the symbols on the obelisk. "It's about balance," she said, her voice filled with urgency. "The elements earth, wind, fire, water, shadow. The Heart is testing our ability to understand the balance of power."

Leo rolled his eyes, flames still flickering in his hands. "Great, so now we have to play a game while a giant rock monster tries to crush us?"

Maya, her connection to the earth pulsing with energy, stepped forward. "No, it's more than that. It's testing whether we can work together to balance our powers, to understand the forces that govern Ravenrode."

Nora nodded, her shadows swirling in response. "It's not about brute strength. It's about understanding the magic that binds this place together."

A Race Against Time

The Guardian moved closer, each step causing the ground to tremble. Finn could feel the pressure mounting. They didn't have much time.

"Alright," he said, his voice steady despite the tension. "We need to figure this out. Sophie, you focus on the obelisk. The rest of us will hold the Guardian back."

Sophie nodded, her mind already working through the symbols. "The elements are the key," she muttered. "We have to channel them into the obelisk each of us focusing on our own power."

Maya stepped forward, placing her hands on the ground. The earth responded to her immediately, vines and roots shooting up from the soil to form a barrier between them and the Guardian. "This should buy us some time," she said, her voice tight with concentration.

Leo, flames licking at his fingertips, moved to stand beside Maya. "I'll add some fire to that," he said, sending streams of flame through the vines, hardening them into a fiery wall. Nora's shadows wove through the flames, strengthening the barrier further. "We're going to need more than this," she said, her eyes flickering with determination. "Sophie, hurry."

Sophie's fingers danced over the obelisk, her mind racing as she deciphered the symbols. "The Heart is connected to the elements," she muttered. "We have to activate them wind, fire, earth, water, and shadow. Each of us has to channel our power into the obelisk at the same time." Finn nodded, his grip on his staff tightening. "We're ready. Let's do this."

The Power of the Elements

As the Guardian pushed against the barrier, the friends moved into position around the obelisk. Sophie stood at the center, guiding them as they prepared to channel their powers into the stone.

Maya was the first to act, her hands pressing into the earth as she summoned the strength of the forest. Vines shot up from the ground, intertwining with the symbols on the obelisk, connecting her energy to the ancient stone.

Leo followed, flames roaring to life in his hands. He directed the fire toward the obelisk, watching as the symbols glowed brighter, reacting to the heat of his power.

Nora's shadows slipped through the cracks in the obelisk, weaving themselves into the symbols like threads of darkness. The air around her grew colder, the shadows merging with the ancient magic of the Heart.

Finn raised his staff, summoning the wind to swirl around them. The air crackled with energy as the wind intertwined with the fire, earth, and shadows, completing the circle.

Sophie, standing at the center of it all, felt the Heart of Ravenrode respond. The symbols on the obelisk flared to life, glowing with a brilliance that lit up the entire clearing. The ground trembled, but this time it wasn't in fear it was in acknowledgment. "We've done it," Sophie whispered, her voice filled with awe.

But the Guardian wasn't finished. It let out a deafening roar, breaking through the barrier and charging toward them with renewed fury.

Chapter 30

The Awakening of Ravenrode

The roar of the Guardian shook the forest to its core. Its massive stone body barreled toward the group, eyes glowing with an intensity that made the ground tremble beneath their feet. The magic of the obelisk flared around them, but it wasn't enough to stop the ancient force from advancing. The Heart of Ravenrode had chosen its test, and the Guardian was its enforcer.

"We need to hold it back!" Finn shouted, his voice barely cutting through the chaos.

Leo clenched his fists, flames erupting from his hands. "I'll keep it busy!" he yelled, launching a fiery wave at the creature. The flames licked across the Guardian's stone body, but the creature barely slowed, its ancient form impervious to the heat.

Maya's voice cut through the panic. "We're not trying to defeat it!" she called, her hands pressed against the earth. "We need to channel more power into the obelisk! The magic is the key, not brute strength!"

Sophie nodded, her eyes fixed on the glowing symbols of the obelisk. "The Guardian is tied to the Heart. It's not just a test of our strength it's testing our connection to the elements!"

Nora's shadows swirled around her as she positioned herself between the Guardian and the group. "We need to show it that we understand the balance of Ravenrode," she said, her voice calm despite the tension. "It won't stop until we prove ourselves worthy."

The Power Within

Maya knelt, her hands digging into the earth, feeling the energy coursing beneath her. The ground pulsed with life, responding to her every touch. "The Heart is alive," she murmured, more to herself than anyone else. "It's watching us, waiting for us to tap into its true power."

Finn's heart raced as the realization hit him. The Heart wasn't just an ancient source of magic it was a living force, connected to every element in Ravenrode. And it wasn't enough to simply fight the Guardian they had to prove that they understood the deeper magic that bound the forest together.

"We have to combine our powers!" Finn shouted. "It's not just about attacking! We need to work together, to show the Heart that we're in balance!"

Sophie's eyes lit up with understanding. "That's it! We need to synchronize our powers, our elements. The Heart is testing our ability to act as one."

Leo frowned, launching another stream of fire at the Guardian to buy them time. "Fine, but how exactly are we supposed to do that?"

Nora, her eyes gleaming with determination, stepped forward. "We connect. Like we did with the obelisk. But this time, we channel the magic directly into the Heart."

The Guardian's steps shook the earth, its form towering over them as it approached. They didn't have much time.

Unleashing the Elements

Maya took a deep breath, closing her eyes as she reached out with her power. The vines beneath her hands pulsed with energy, growing stronger as they wrapped around the obelisk. "Earth is my anchor," she whispered, her voice steady. "I can feel the pulse of the forest the Heart is waiting for us."

Finn stepped beside her, raising his staff. The wind answered his call, swirling around them in a fierce gust. "Wind will carry us forward," he said, his voice filled with conviction. "Together, we'll harness the storm."

Leo, his fiery confidence blazing, nodded. "Fire will light the way." He planted his feet firmly on the ground, his flames intertwining with the swirling winds, adding heat and strength to the gathering energy.

Nora stood at the edge of the group, her shadows coiling like living entities. "And shadows will bind us," she said, her voice soft but firm. The darkness wove itself around the flames and the wind, creating a delicate balance between light and dark.

Sophie, standing at the center, placed her hands on the obelisk, her fingers tracing the ancient symbols that glowed with an almost sentient energy. "Life will unite us," she said, her voice resonating with the magic of the forest. The plants and animals of Ravenrode seemed to respond to her words, the very air thrumming with life.

The five friends stood as one, their powers converging into a single, unified force. The magic of the elements surged around them, pulsing with the heartbeat of the forest itself.

The Heart's Response

The Guardian, sensing the shift in the magic, hesitated for the first time. Its glowing eyes dimmed slightly as it paused, watching the group with a newfound intensity. The air around it crackled with energy, but it didn't attack.

The obelisk began to hum, a deep, resonant sound that echoed through the clearing. The symbols on its surface flared with light, glowing brighter and brighter as the magic of the elements flowed into it.

"We're doing it," Sophie whispered, her eyes wide with awe. "The Heart is responding."

But the test wasn't over yet. As the obelisk pulsed with power, the ground beneath them rumbled, and a deep, ancient voice filled the air.

"You have unlocked the first path," the voice said, its tone low and rumbling, like the earth itself was speaking. "But the Heart of Ravenrode is more than just power. It is balance, life, and death. To claim its secrets, you must prove your understanding of all."

The Guardian stepped back, its form dissolving into the earth as if it had never been there. The air grew still, and the obelisk's glow faded, leaving the group standing in silence.

"What... just happened?" Leo asked, his voice filled with disbelief.

"We passed the test," Finn said, his eyes still fixed on the obelisk. "But there's more to this. The Heart isn't just a source of power it's a living force. And it's testing us in ways we don't fully understand yet."

Nora's shadows flickered at her feet as she glanced around the clearing. "The Guardian was just the beginning. There are more tests waiting for us. We're not done here."

The Deeper Mystery

Sophie stepped closer to the obelisk, her hand resting on its smooth surface. "The Heart is watching us," she murmured. "But it's not just testing our powers. It's testing our understanding of the magic that binds this place together."

Maya nodded, her connection to the earth still pulsing beneath her feet. "The forest, the elements, the shadows they're all part of something bigger. Something we haven't fully uncovered yet."

Leo, still buzzing with adrenaline from the fight, ran a hand through his hair. "Great. So, what's next? Another giant monster? A cryptic puzzle?"

Finn shook his head, his mind racing. "No, it's not about fighting or solving riddles. The Heart wants us to understand something fundamental about Ravenrode something that goes beyond the magic we've learned so far."

Nora's eyes flickered with intensity. "Then we need to go deeper. We need to uncover the true purpose of the Heart."

Sophie nodded, her gaze never leaving the obelisk. "And we need to be ready for whatever comes next."

A New Path

The air in the clearing had changed. It no longer felt oppressive or threatening, but there was still a sense of mystery lingering around them. The Heart of Ravenrode had accepted their first trial, but it was clear that this was only the beginning.

As the group prepared to leave the clearing, Finn glanced over his shoulder at the obelisk one last time. The symbols on its surface had faded, but the magic was still there quiet, waiting.

"We're not done here," Finn said, his voice low but filled with resolve. "The Heart has more to show us. And we're going to find out what it is."

The friends exchanged determined glances, knowing that the true test was still ahead. The magic of Ravenrode ran deeper than any of them had imagined, and the mysteries of the Heart were far from being fully revealed.

With renewed purpose, they set off through the forest once more, ready to face whatever trials lay ahead.

But as they disappeared into the trees, the Heart of Ravenrode pulsed one last time its ancient power stirring, watching, and waiting for them to return.

Chapter 31

The Forest's Secrets

The deeper they ventured into the forest, the more the air seemed to thrum with magic. The trees, tall and ancient, closed in around them, their thick branches casting long shadows on the path. The Heart of Ravenrode had spoken, but its message had only opened more questions. What did it mean by "balance, life, and death"? What was the true purpose of the Heart?

Sophie led the way, her mind racing. The obelisk, the Guardian, the strange voice it all pointed to something far greater than any of them had anticipated. As they walked, she couldn't shake the feeling that they were being watched, not by a creature or a person, but by the forest itself.

"We need to figure out what the Heart is hiding," Finn said, breaking the silence. "The tests, the puzzles it's all leading us somewhere."

"But where?" Leo asked, his tone filled with frustration. "We passed the first trial, and now what? Another cryptic clue? Another monster waiting to test us?"

Nora, who had been walking at the back, spoke quietly. "It's not just about power. The Heart is more than just a magical force. It's testing us because it wants something from us something more than strength."

Maya nodded. "It's about understanding. We're not just here to unlock some ancient magic. We're here to uncover the truth about Ravenrode."

Finn glanced at Maya. "What kind of truth?"

Maya didn't answer right away, her eyes scanning the forest as if searching for something. "The elements, the shadows, the earth everything here is connected. The Heart isn't just a source of magic. It's the source of life in this forest. And I think... it's trying to protect something."

An Uneasy Feeling

As they walked, the path before them grew narrower, the trees thicker, their branches knotted together like gnarled fingers. The air was cooler now, and a mist had begun to settle over the ground, swirling around their feet.

"I don't like this," Leo muttered, his flames sparking to life in his hands. "It feels like we're walking into a trap."

Sophie shook her head. "It's not a trap. The forest isn't trying to hurt us it's trying to show us something."

Nora, her eyes sharp, whispered, "The shadows are different here. They're... watching us."

Finn tightened his grip on his staff, his wind magic stirring slightly. "We need to stay alert. Whatever the Heart is leading us to, it's not going to be easy."

They pressed on, each of them tense and ready for anything. The mist grew thicker as they descended into a small valley, the trees on either side towering like sentinels. There was something about this part of the forest that felt different older, more powerful.

Sophie suddenly stopped, her eyes fixed on something up ahead. "Do you see that?" she whispered.

The others followed her gaze. Through the mist, a large stone archway stood, half-hidden by vines and moss. The arch was ancient, its surface worn by time, but faint carvings could still be seen etched into the stone.

Leo frowned. "What is this place?"

Maya stepped closer, running her fingers over the carvings. "It's a doorway. But to where?"

Finn, his heart pounding, stepped forward. "We need to find out."

The stone archway loomed over them, and as they approached, the carvings began to glow faintly, much like the symbols on the obelisk. Sophie knelt before the base of the arch, her fingers brushing the ancient symbols.

"These are different from the ones on the obelisk," she murmured. "But they're connected. This is another part of the Heart's puzzle."

Nora stood back, watching the shadows that seemed to dance at the edges of the arch. "This place is dangerous. Whatever lies beyond that doorway, it's not meant to be found."

"We don't have a choice," Finn said. "If we're going to understand the Heart, we need to go through."

Maya, her connection to the earth humming beneath her feet, nodded. "I can feel it. This doorway leads to something important. Something buried deep within the forest."

With a deep breath, Sophie stood and placed her hands on the stone arch. The symbols glowed brighter, and a low rumble echoed through the valley. The ground beneath them shook slightly, and the mist seemed to part, revealing the path ahead.

Leo, ever the brave one, stepped forward first. "Well, here goes nothing," he said, his flames flickering in his hands as he passed under the arch.

One by one, the others followed, their hearts racing. As they stepped through the archway, the world around them seemed to shift. The mist thickened, the trees grew taller, and the very air felt different heavier, as though they had stepped into a place where time itself had slowed.

The Lost Grove

On the other side of the archway was a vast clearing, unlike anything they had ever seen. The trees here were ancient, their bark silver and smooth, their leaves a deep, shimmering green. The ground was covered in thick moss, and in the center of the clearing stood a massive stone circle, much like the one they had encountered earlier, but far more intricate.

"The Lost Grove," Maya whispered, her voice filled with awe. "This place is... alive."

Sophie nodded, her eyes wide. "The Heart of Ravenrode... it's connected to this place. The magic here is stronger, older."

Nora's gaze swept across the clearing, her eyes narrowed. "There's something else here."

Suddenly, the ground trembled, and a low, resonant hum filled the air. The stone circle in the center of the clearing began to glow, and from the shadows at the edge of the grove, a figure emerged. It was tall, cloaked in darkness, its face hidden beneath a hood.

The figure's voice was deep, echoing through the grove. "You have come far, but you are not yet ready. The Heart of Ravenrode holds many secrets that you are not yet prepared to uncover."

Finn stepped forward, his eyes blazing with determination. "We're here to learn. We're ready."

The figure shook its head. "The Heart is not a prize to be claimed. It is a living force, bound to this land. And those who seek its power must prove their worth."

Leo raised his flames defensively. "We've already passed your tests. What more do you want from us?"

The figure's voice grew softer, but no less powerful. "The trials of Ravenrode are not about strength or power. They are about understanding. Only those who truly understand the balance of life and death, of creation and destruction, will be allowed to proceed."

Sophie's heart raced. "And if we fail?" The figure's eyes gleamed from beneath its hood. "Then the Heart will remain hidden, and the darkness within will rise."

The Second Trial

Without warning, the figure raised its hand, and the ground beneath their feet shifted. The moss parted, revealing a swirling pool of dark water in the center of the stone circle. The air around them grew colder, and the trees seemed to lean in closer, as though the forest itself was watching.

"This is your second trial," the figure said. "The Trial of Reflection. Step into the waters, and face the truth of who you are. Only by confronting your darkest selves can you move forward."

Nora's shadows flickered around her feet. "This is a trap," she muttered. "The waters aren't just magic they're alive."

Finn nodded, but his resolve didn't falter. "It doesn't matter. If this is the only way to uncover the truth about the Heart, we'll do it."

Sophie stepped forward, her eyes fixed on the dark water. "We have no other choice."

Maya, her connection to the earth stronger than ever, knelt beside the pool. "The water... it's tied to the Heart. But there's something beneath it. Something hidden."

Leo, his flames dimmed, stared at the water with unease. "Whatever it is, we're about to find out."

Without another word, Finn stepped into the pool. The water rippled around him, and for a moment, nothing happened. But then, the surface of the water began to glow, and the reflection that stared back at him wasn't his own it was something darker, something twisted.

The others watched in silence as Finn's reflection shifted, showing him visions of his past, of choices he hadn't made, of paths he hadn't taken. It was a glimpse into the darkest parts of himself his fears, his regrets, his doubts.

Sophie, Leo, Maya, and Nora followed, each of them stepping into the pool and facing their own reflections. The water rippled with magic, showing each of them their deepest fears, their darkest memories.

But the test wasn't just about fear. It was about acceptance about facing the parts of themselves they had tried to bury.

Chapter 32

Reflections in the Dark

The air around them seemed to tighten as the group stepped into the cold waters of the pool, its surface rippling with an ancient, magical energy. Each of them felt the weight of the magic, but more than that, they felt the pull something deeper than mere reflection. The water seemed to draw out their thoughts, their memories, and their darkest selves, laying them bare for all to see.

Finn was the first to feel the change. As he stared into the pool, his own reflection blurred and twisted until it was no longer him staring back. Instead, a version of himself emerged harder, colder, his face lined with anger and doubt. The reflection spoke, its voice low and venomous.

"Do you really think you can lead them?" it hissed, its eyes narrowing with disdain. "You've never been strong enough. You've always doubted yourself, always afraid to make the tough choices. They follow you now, but when it really matters, you'll fail them."

Finn's heart raced, but he stood his ground. "I won't fail," he whispered, though his voice trembled. "I can't."

The reflection smirked, its dark eyes gleaming. "You say that, but deep down, you know the truth. You're not the leader they think you are. You're not ready."

Sophie's Reflection

Sophie stood beside Finn, her eyes locked on her own reflection. At first, the water showed only her face, calm and steady. But then it shifted, and the reflection that stared back was full of fear her eyes wide with uncertainty, her face pale and strained.

"You don't belong here," the reflection whispered. "You've always known that. You're not like the others. You don't have the strength or the courage to face what's coming. You're weak."

Sophie's chest tightened, the words cutting deep. She had always tried to push those thoughts away, but hearing them spoken aloud by her own reflection made them feel real. "I'm not weak," she said softly, though doubt laced her words. "I've fought just as hard as the others."

"But you're not like them," the reflection continued. "You rely on them to protect you. You hide behind your powers, pretending to be strong, but you know that when it comes down to it, you'll fail. And they'll suffer because of you."

Sophie clenched her fists, her mind racing. "I won't let that happen," she whispered, but the fear lingered.

Leo's Reflection

Leo, always the one to confront things head-on, stared into the water, expecting something fierce. But what he saw shocked him more than anything else could have. His reflection wasn't full of anger or fire it was hollow. The flames that usually burned so brightly within him were dimmed, his face lined with uncertainty.

"You think you're strong," the reflection said, its voice quiet but biting. "But you're just a show-off. You use your fire to hide the fact that you're scared. Scared of what people will see if they look too closely."

Leo's jaw tightened, his hands balling into fists. "I'm not scared," he growled.

The reflection smirked. "Aren't you? You hide behind your fire, pretending to be brave, but deep down, you're afraid. Afraid that one day, your fire will burn out, and you'll be nothing."

Leo's heart pounded in his chest. He had always pushed his doubts aside, covering them with confidence and bravado. But now, facing his reflection, he couldn't ignore the fear gnawing at him. What if he wasn't as strong as he thought?

Maya's Reflection

Maya stood beside the others, her reflection swirling in the dark water. At first, it seemed calm, as she always was, but then it shifted, showing a version of herself that was uncertain, lost.

"You don't know where you belong," the reflection whispered. "You pretend to be the steady one, the calm one, but you've always felt out of place. You've never truly known your purpose."

Maya's breath caught in her throat. She had always been the one to keep things together, the one who stayed level-headed when everyone else panicked. But the reflection was right there had always been a part of her that felt disconnected, unsure of where she fit in the world.

"You're a follower," the reflection continued. "You follow Finn, follow the others, because you don't know how to lead. You don't know what your role is, do you?"

Maya's heart ached with the truth of the words. "I do know," she whispered, though her voice was shaky. "I help keep us together."

The reflection smiled, cold and cruel. "But is that enough?"

Nora's Reflection

Nora was the last to face the water, and as she looked down, her reflection was already distorted, twisted by shadows that coiled around her like smoke. Her reflection didn't speak at first it simply stared at her, its dark eyes filled with something Nora recognized all too well: fear.

"You hide in the shadows," the reflection finally whispered. "You think they make you strong. But all they do is hide the truth. You're scared of what you'll find if you step out of the darkness."

Nora's breath caught in her throat. The shadows had always been her strength, her shield. But the reflection's words hit too close to home. "I'm not hiding," she said, though her voice wavered.

"Yes, you are," the reflection hissed. "You use the shadows to avoid the truth. You're afraid of what you might see if you let the light in."

Nora's hands trembled as she stared at the twisted version of herself. She had always felt safe in the darkness, but now, for the first time, she wondered if the shadows were hiding more than just her fears.

The Test of Acceptance

The group stood in silence, each of them confronting their own reflection, their own fears laid bare. The dark water rippled around them, showing them the darkest parts of themselves, the parts they had tried so hard to hide.

"This is the test," Finn said quietly, his voice steady despite the weight of his words. "The Heart isn't just testing our power. It's testing if we can accept who we are."

Sophie nodded, her heart heavy with the truth. "We have to face it our fears, our doubts. We have to accept them."

Leo's flames flickered weakly as he stared into the water. "It's not just about being strong, is it? It's about understanding that we're more than just our power."

Maya closed her eyes, her connection to the earth grounding her. "Balance," she whispered. "It's about balance."

Nora's shadows flickered around her as she took a deep breath. "We have to embrace all of it the light and the dark."

One by one, they stood taller, their resolve growing stronger. The reflections in the water didn't disappear, but the fear in their eyes began to fade. They were still there the doubts, the fears but now, they weren't running from them.

"We can't be perfect," Finn said, his voice filled with determination. "But we can be stronger because of our flaws."

Sophie smiled faintly. "And we can be stronger together."

The Waters Recede

As the group stood united, the dark waters began to ripple once more. The reflections in the water shifted, slowly fading until only their true selves remained. The cold air lifted, and the oppressive weight of the trial began to ease.

The voice of the figure echoed through the grove once more. "You have faced your darkest selves, and yet you stand. The Heart of Ravenrode is not just power it is understanding. And now, you have taken the first step."

The waters of the pool stilled, and the mist that had surrounded them began to dissipate. The figure at the edge of the clearing remained, watching them with unreadable eyes.

"You are not yet ready," the figure said, its voice softer now. "But you are closer than you were. The Heart will reveal its secrets to those who prove they are worthy. But beware there is still darkness to come."

With those words, the figure dissolved into the shadows, leaving the group standing in the now-still grove.

A New Understanding

The friends stood in silence for a moment, the weight of the trial still heavy in their hearts. Each of them had faced something difficult something personal. But now, there was a sense of relief, as though a burden had been lifted.

"We did it," Finn said, his voice quiet but firm. "We passed the trial."

Sophie nodded, though her mind was still racing. "But what comes next?"

Leo let out a breath, his flames now a steady glow. "Whatever it is, we'll face it. Together."

Maya, her connection to the earth still pulsing beneath her feet, glanced around the grove. "We're not done yet. The Heart still has more to show us."

Nora's shadows flickered at her feet, but there was a new light in her eyes. "And we'll be ready."

With that, they turned back toward the path, knowing that this was only the beginning. The Heart of Ravenrode had many more secrets to reveal and they were ready to uncover them.

Chapter 33

The Path Beyond

The mist that had once enveloped the grove was gone, and the air around them felt clearer, lighter, but still charged with the lingering magic of the Heart. The five friends, having faced their darkest selves, walked away from the pool with a newfound resolve. The journey had taken an unexpected turn this was no longer just about unlocking the magic of Ravenrode. It was about understanding the very nature of the power they sought and how it connected to them in ways they hadn't realized before.

Finn walked ahead, his gaze focused but thoughtful. The weight of leadership pressed on him more than ever after facing the reflection of his doubts. He had always been the one to lead them, to push them forward but now, more than ever, he understood the importance of leaning on the others. They weren't just following him. They were all part of something bigger.

"We've passed the first two trials," Sophie said, breaking the silence as they moved deeper into the forest. "But something tells me the hardest one is still ahead of us."

Nora nodded, her shadows flickering as she glanced around. "The Heart isn't done with us. There's more it wants to show. More it wants us to understand."

Leo, ever restless, let a flicker of flame dance between his fingers as they walked. "So, what's next? Another ancient Guardian? A cryptic riddle that doesn't make sense?"

Maya, walking with calm determination, placed a hand on the ground, feeling the earth pulse beneath her feet. "I think we're getting closer to something deeper. The magic is changing."

Finn stopped and turned to face the group. "Whatever next, we'll face it together. We've come too far to back down now."

The others nodded in agreement, but the tension in the air was undeniable. The Heart had already tested their strength and their understanding of themselves. Now, it felt as though the final test would challenge their unity, their bond.

The Marked Path

As they continued, the landscape around them shifted. The trees grew taller, their trunks wider and their branches more twisted. The air became colder, sharper, and the ground beneath their feet felt rougher, less welcoming. The deeper they ventured, the more they felt the pull of the Heart drawing them toward something ancient, something hidden beneath the surface.

Maya stopped suddenly, her eyes narrowing as she looked ahead. "There's something carved into the ground."

The group gathered around the spot she had pointed to. Deep, intricate markings were etched into the earth, forming a large, circular symbol. It was similar to the ones they had seen before, but these markings were different older, more elaborate.

"These symbols..." Sophie knelt down to study them. "They're not like the ones on the obelisk. This is something else. A gateway, maybe?"

Nora crouched beside her, her fingers tracing the lines of the symbol. "It's a boundary," she said softly. "Something's being kept inside."

Finn's heart quickened. "Or something's being kept out."

Leo's flames flickered brighter. "Either way, it looks like we're about to find out."

Sophie stood, her gaze shifting to the dense forest beyond the circle. "I think this is the final trial. Whatever lies beyond this boundary it's what the Heart has been leading us to."

Maya, always grounded in the moment, placed a hand on Sophie's shoulder. "Are we ready for this?"

Sophie nodded, though the uncertainty in her eyes was clear. "We have to be."

Crossing the Boundary

The air seemed to change the moment they stepped across the boundary. It was subtle at first a shift in the temperature, a slight change in the way the wind moved through the trees but as they walked further, it became undeniable. The magic here was different. Stronger, darker.

"We're not in Ravenrode anymore," Leo muttered, his voice barely above a whisper.

Finn agreed. The forest felt alien, like a place that didn't belong to the world they knew. It was as though they had stepped into a different realm, a place where the rules of nature didn't apply. The trees here were taller, their branches twisting into shapes that resembled claws. The ground was uneven, littered with strange stones that glowed faintly in the fading light.

"We're being watched," Nora said, her voice low but calm. The shadows at her feet seemed to flicker with life, as if responding to the presence around them. "Something's here."

Sophie's heart raced as she looked around. The air felt thick, like the weight of a thousand eyes was on them. She could feel the magic in her bones, humming with an intensity that both excited and terrified her.

"What is this place?" Maya whispered, her connection to the earth strained as she tried to sense what lay beneath their feet. But even the earth here felt wrong, as if it were hiding its true nature.

"The final trial," Finn said, his voice steady but tense. "This is where the Heart of Ravenrode will decide if we're worthy."

The Presence

As they moved deeper into the heart of the strange forest, the feeling of being watched grew stronger. The trees seemed to shift, their branches creaking as if they were alive, observing the group's every move. The wind howled through the leaves, carrying with it a faint, distant whisper that none of them could quite make out.

Suddenly, the ground beneath their feet trembled, and a low rumbling echoed through the trees. The wind died down, and the air grew deathly still. Finn tightened his grip on his staff, his instincts screaming that something was coming.

"We're not alone," Leo muttered, his flames flaring to life as he prepared for whatever was about to emerge from the darkness.

From the shadows ahead, a figure appeared. At first, it was just a silhouette, barely visible in the dim light, but as it stepped closer, the group could see that it wasn't human. It was tall, with a body that seemed to be made of smoke and shadow, its form shifting and changing as it moved.

Its eyes glowing red and full of ancient knowledge locked onto the group, and the air around them seemed to grow heavier, as though the presence of the creature itself weighed on their very souls.

The figure stopped a few feet away, and when it spoke, its voice was like the wind through the trees soft, yet filled with power. "You have come far," it said, its eyes scanning each of them. "But the Heart of Ravenrode does not give its secrets freely."

Sophie stepped forward, her heart pounding in her chest. "We've passed your tests. We've faced our fears. What more do you want from us?"

The figure's eyes glowed brighter, and it seemed to smile, though its face remained obscured by shadow. "You have faced yourselves, yes. But now, you must face the truth."

The Trial of Truth

Before any of them could respond, the figure raised its hand, and the ground beneath them split open. A deep, dark chasm yawned at their feet, and from it rose a blinding light. The light wasn't warm or comforting it was cold, sharp, and filled with a truth so powerful that it seemed to cut through the very air.

The figure's voice echoed through the clearing. "Step into the light, and you will see the truth of the Heart. But be warned once you see, you cannot unsee."

Finn's breath caught in his throat. The light called to him, but there was a part of him that feared what it would reveal. What truth would the Heart show them? And were they ready to face it?

Sophie reached out and took Finn's hand, her grip steady despite the fear in her eyes. "We have to do this," she whispered. "We came this far for answers."

Maya nodded, her face set with determination. "Whatever it is, we face it together."

Leo's flames flared brighter as he stared into the light. "Let's do this."

Nora, her shadows coiling around her, took a deep breath. "We're ready."

With one final glance at each other, they stepped forward into the light.

Chapter 34

The Truth Unveiled

As they stepped into the blinding light, the world around them seemed to dissolve. The forest, the strange figure, even the ground beneath their feet everything faded away, leaving only the light. It enveloped them completely, its cold, sharp brilliance cutting through their senses like a blade. For a moment, there was nothing but the light and the overwhelming sensation of being laid bare, as if the magic of the Heart was stripping away every layer of their being.

Finn's heart raced as he felt the light reach deep inside him, pulling at something buried within something he had long tried to ignore. His breath caught in his throat as a vision began to take shape before him.

Finn's Vision: The Weight of Leadership

In the vision, Finn stood alone on a cliff overlooking a vast, stormy ocean. The wind whipped around him, pulling at his clothes, and the sky above was dark, swirling with ominous clouds. Lightning crackled in the distance, and the roar of thunder echoed through the air. He could feel the power of the storm, but there was something else a sense of overwhelming responsibility.

Suddenly, figures appeared behind him his friends. Sophie, Maya, Leo, and Nora stood there, their faces filled with expectation. They were looking to him for guidance, for strength, but Finn felt the crushing weight of their trust pressing down on him.

"You're not ready," a voice whispered in his ear. The voice was familiar his own doubts, the ones that had haunted him for as long as he could remember. "You can't lead them. You'll fail, and when you do, they'll suffer for it."

Finn's fists clenched, his knuckles white. The storm around him grew fiercer, the wind howling in his ears. "I won't fail them," he said, though his voice trembled. "I can't."

The voice laughed, low and mocking. "You doubt yourself. And your doubt will be your undoing."

The vision shifted, and suddenly, Finn was alone again. The cliff crumbled beneath him, and he fell, spiraling into the darkness below. The wind howled louder, but this time, it didn't obey him. It was wild, uncontrollable, and Finn was powerless against it.

Sophie's Vision: The Fear of Weakness

Sophie stood in a dense, overgrown forest. The trees around her were tall and twisted, their branches forming a dark canopy overhead. She felt small, insignificant, as though the forest itself was swallowing her whole. The plants and vines that she had always commanded now seemed foreign, resistant to her touch. When she reached out, the leaves crumbled in her hands, turning to ash.

"You don't belong here," the voice echoed through the trees, cold and sharp. "You're not like them. You're weak, Sophie. You've always been weak."

Sophie's breath hitched, her heart pounding in her chest. "I'm not weak," she whispered, but the words felt hollow.

The forest around her grew darker, the trees closing in. From the shadows, dark figures emerged twisted, grotesque versions of the creatures she once controlled. They snarled and growled, their eyes glowing with malice as they surrounded her.

"You can't control them," the voice taunted. "You can't even control yourself. You rely on the others to protect you. Without them, you're nothing."

Sophie's chest tightened, fear gripping her like a vice. "I'm not nothing," she said, but the doubt gnawed at her.

The figures drew closer, their snarling faces inches from hers. Sophie tried to summon her magic, tried to command the plants to protect her, but nothing happened. The ground beneath her feet crumbled, and she fell into the dark earth, sinking deeper and deeper until there was nothing but silence.

Leo's Vision: The Fear of Losing Control

Leo found himself standing in a barren wasteland, the sky above him a dull, oppressive gray. The air was dry, hot, and suffocating, and the ground beneath his feet was cracked and

scorched. Flames flickered around him, but they were weak, dim nothing like the roaring inferno he was used to.

"You've lost it," the voice said, cold and mocking. "Your fire is gone, Leo. Without it, you're nothing."

Leo's fists clenched, his hands trembling as he tried to summon the flames. But nothing happened. The fire inside him had always been his greatest strength, his source of power and confidence. But now, it was gone, leaving him feeling empty, hollow.

"You hide behind your fire," the voice continued. "But without it, you're just scared. You've always been scared."

"No," Leo growled, but the fear gnawed at him. The flames flickered weakly at his fingertips, but they wouldn't come to life.

The wasteland around him grew darker, colder. The ground cracked open, and from the fissures, tendrils of darkness slithered toward him, wrapping around his legs, pulling him down into the earth. Leo struggled, but without his fire, he was powerless.

"You're nothing without the flames," the voice hissed, and Leo felt the ground give way beneath him, plunging him into the darkness.

Maya's Vision: The Fear of Not Belonging

Maya stood at the edge of a vast, empty desert. The sky above her was endless, stretching out into infinity, but the land around her was barren, lifeless. She felt small, insignificant, as though she were nothing more than a speck in the vastness of the world.

"You've never known where you belong," the voice whispered, carried on the wind. "You pretend to be strong, to keep everyone together, but deep down, you know the truth. You don't fit in."

Maya's heart ached with the weight of the words. She had always tried to be the steady one, the calm one, but there had always been a part of her that felt disconnected, out of place.

The desert stretched out before her, vast and empty, and Maya felt a deep sense of loneliness wash over her. The ground beneath her feet was dry and cracked, and when she reached down to touch the earth, it crumbled in her hands.

"You don't belong," the voice said again, and Maya felt the ground give way beneath her, pulling her down into the void.

Nora's Vision: The Fear of the Light

Nora stood in a world of shadows, the darkness swirling around her like a living thing. She had always found comfort in the shadows, had always felt at home in the darkness. But now, the shadows felt different heavier, more oppressive.

"You hide in the darkness," the voice whispered, soft and cold. "But the truth is, you're afraid. You're afraid of what you'll see if you step into the light."

Nora's breath hitched. The shadows had always been her shield, her protection. But the voice's words struck a chord deep within her.

"You think the darkness makes you strong," the voice continued, "but it's just hiding your fear."

Suddenly, a bright light pierced the shadows, and Nora flinched, stepping back instinctively. The light was blinding, sharp, and it cut through the darkness like a knife. For the first time, Nora felt exposed, vulnerable.

"You're afraid of the light," the voice said, and the shadows around Nora began to dissolve, leaving her standing in the harsh, unforgiving light.
The Truth of the Heart

The visions faded, and the group found themselves back in the clearing, the blinding light of the chasm still glowing beneath them. The figure of shadow stood before them, watching in silence as they struggled to catch their breath, their hearts pounding with the weight of what they had just seen.

"The Heart of Ravenrode is not just power," the figure said, its voice softer now. "It is truth. And the truth is not always easy to face."

Finn looked at his friends, seeing the strain in their faces, the weight of their own truths pressing down on them. But they were still standing. They had faced the darkest parts of themselves, and they had survived.

"We're not perfect," Finn said, his voice steady despite the lingering fear in his heart. "But we're still here. And we're not backing down."

Sophie stepped forward, her eyes filled with determination. "We've seen the truth. We've faced it. Now, what comes next?"

The figure's eyes gleamed, and it slowly raised its hand. "The Heart has revealed its truth to you. But there is one final test."

The ground beneath them trembled once more, and the chasm widened. From its depths, a blinding light shot into the sky, and the figure's voice echoed through the clearing.

"You must prove that you can control the power of the Heart. Only then will you be worthy."

Chapter 35

The Path Forward

The light from the chasm flickered and then faded, leaving the group standing in the eerie silence of the forest. The figure, which had loomed over them, watching their every move, dissolved into the shadows without a word. For the first time since stepping into this realm of the Heart, the oppressive weight that had been pressing down on them seemed to lift.

The final test had been spoken of, but now it felt as if they were standing on the edge of something else entirely—a path forward that wasn't defined by trials or confrontations, but by choice.

Finn took a deep breath, steadying himself. The visions had shaken him, as they had shaken them all. But standing here now, he felt a strange clarity. "That's it," he said, his voice breaking the silence. "No more tests."

Sophie glanced at him, her brow furrowed in confusion. "What do you mean?"

"We're done playing its game," Finn replied, looking around at the others. "The Heart has shown us what it wanted us to see. We've faced our fears, our doubts. We don't need to keep proving ourselves."

Maya knelt and pressed her hand against the earth. The ground beneath her pulsed with a subtle energy, not the overpowering force of earlier, but something gentler, quieter. "The forest feels... different now," she said. "Like it's no longer trying to challenge us."

Leo, always the first to take action, walked forward and peered down into the now-quiet chasm. "So, what do we do now?" he asked, flames still flickering at his fingertips. "Just walk away?"

Nora's shadows swirled around her feet as she studied the darkness beyond the clearing. "No," she said quietly. "The Heart has shown us its secrets. It's not about passing tests anymore. It's about what we choose to do next."

A Choice to Make

The group stood in silence, absorbing Nora's words. There was no longer the sense that something was pushing them forward, no unseen force urging them into the next trial. Instead, they were left with a choice—a decision that would shape the path ahead.

Sophie stepped closer to the chasm, staring down into its depths. "The Heart is more than just magic," she murmured. "It's alive. It's part of this place, part of us."

Finn nodded, his heart pounding in his chest as he realized what Sophie was saying. "It's not about controlling the Heart," he said. "It's about understanding it. We were never meant to conquer it or prove ourselves worthy. We were meant to protect it."

Maya stood, brushing her hands against her legs as she looked at the group. "The Heart of Ravenrode isn't just a source of power—it's the life force of this entire forest. And it's been calling out to us because something is threatening it."

Leo crossed his arms, his flames dimming as he listened. "So, all of this—the tests, the trials—they were just to get us here? To make us realize that we have a responsibility to this place?"

"Yes," Sophie said, her voice filled with certainty. "The Heart wanted us to see the truth—not just about ourselves, but about Ravenrode . There's something bigger happening here, something we need to stop."

Nora, her shadows dancing at her fingertips, glanced at the others. "The darkness we've been sensing—it's coming for the Heart. And if it succeeds,   Ravenrode will fall."

The Darkness Approaches

As if in response to Nora's words, a cold wind swept through the clearing, rustling the leaves and stirring the branches overhead. The warmth that had settled over the forest began to fade, replaced by an icy chill that crept through the air.

"The darkness," Maya whispered, her eyes scanning the trees. "It's coming."

Finn's grip on his staff tightened. "We need to move. We have to protect the Heart."

Sophie turned to him, her eyes wide with urgency. "But how? We still don't fully understand what we're dealing with."

"We don't have time to figure it all out," Leo said, flames flickering to life in his hands once more. "Whatever's coming, we need to stop it. Now."

Nora's gaze darkened as she felt the shadows closing in around them. "This isn't just about protecting the Heart. It's about protecting   Ravenrode . If we fail, everything will fall."

Maya's connection to the earth pulsed with intensity as she knelt once again, pressing her hand to the ground. "There's something moving beneath us," she said, her voice strained. "Something big."

Finn glanced around at his friends, seeing the determination in their faces. They had come this far, and now they had a clear purpose. Protect the Heart. Protect Ravenrode .

"We don't need tests," Finn said, his voice steady. "We need to fight."

A New Purpose

The friends turned toward the forest, their hearts pounding with the weight of the task before them. The magic of the Heart still pulsed beneath their feet, but now it felt like an ally, not an obstacle. It had shown them what they needed to see—about themselves, about the darkness that threatened their home. And now, it was time to act.

"We don't know exactly what's coming," Finn said, gripping his staff tightly. "But we know it's tied to the Heart. Whatever this darkness is, it's been building for a long time."

Leo's flames flared brighter, his confidence returning. "Let it come. We'll burn it down."

Sophie, always the strategist, looked at the group with determination. "We need to find the source of the darkness. If we can stop it before it reaches the Heart, we might still have a chance."

Maya stood, her connection to the earth stronger than ever. "The magic of this place is on our side now. We can use it to our advantage."

Nora, her shadows flickering at her feet, nodded. "We'll protect the Heart. No matter what."

With a final glance at each other, the group set off through the forest, their path clear. The trials were over, and now, they were no longer just students of the magic of Ravenrode . They were its guardians, protectors of a force older and more powerful than any of them had realized.

The Heart had revealed its secrets, and now it was up to them to ensure its survival.

The Gathering Storm

As they moved deeper into the forest, the air grew colder, sharper. The once-familiar trees seemed twisted, darker, and the ground beneath their feet felt unstable, as though the earth itself was holding its breath.

"The darkness is close," Nora said quietly, her shadows coiling around her like a protective cloak.

Finn's heart raced as he sensed the storm building on the horizon. "We'll face it head-on," he said, determination filling his voice. "Together."

Sophie, her mind racing, looked up at the sky. The clouds were thickening, and the wind had taken on a strange, unnatural quality. "We need to move fast," she said. "Whatever this is, it's coming for the Heart—and for us."

Maya pressed her hand to the ground once more, her connection to the earth pulsing through her. "We're not alone," she said, her voice filled with quiet certainty. "The magic of Ravenrode is with us."

Leo, flames dancing at his fingertips, grinned. "Good. We'll need all the help we can get."

As they pushed forward, the storm on the horizon began to take shape. Dark clouds swirled above them, and the wind howled through the trees. The darkness that had been

lurking in the shadows was no longer hiding. It was coming for them, and the Heart was at the center of it all.

But this time, they were ready.

Chapter 36

The Rising Darkness

The forest seemed to close in around them as they pressed forward, the air growing colder with every step. The once vibrant magic of Ravenerode now felt distant, like a quiet murmur beneath the ground. Above them, the dark clouds thickened, swirling in unnatural patterns, and the wind howled through the trees with an ominous force.

Finn led the way, his staff gripped tightly in his hand, the wind at his back. He could feel the storm building, but this time it wasn't one he could control. The darkness they had sensed for so long was finally closing in.

"We're getting closer," Maya said, her voice strained as she pressed her hand to the ground. "The earth feels unstable... like something is breaking through."

Sophie glanced at her, worry flashing across her face. "The Heart's magic isn't strong enough to hold it back on its own."

Leo's flames flickered brightly at his fingertips as he scanned the forest ahead. "Then we're just going to have to make sure this thing never gets close enough to the Heart."

Nora's shadows twisted and curled around her, her eyes sharp and focused. "We don't know what we're dealing with yet. We need to be ready for anything."

The air around them grew thicker, darker, as if the very forest itself was suffocating under the weight of the approaching darkness. They could feel it now—something ancient, something powerful, lurking just beyond the horizon.

The First Sign

As they pushed deeper into the forest, the ground beneath their feet began to shift. The trees, once towering and vibrant, seemed to bend unnaturally, their branches twisting into grotesque shapes. The air was heavy with tension, and a low, resonant hum echoed through the trees, like the sound of something stirring beneath the surface.

Maya stopped abruptly, her eyes wide as she pressed her hands to the ground. "It's moving," she said, her voice barely above a whisper. "The darkness... it's not just coming. It's alive."

Finn's heart pounded in his chest. "We need to keep moving. The Heart is still our only chance."

But before they could take another step, the ground beneath them shook violently, and from the earth, tendrils of dark mist erupted, swirling around their feet. The mist coiled like serpents, creeping toward them with a sinister purpose.

Sophie reacted quickly, raising her hands and summoning vines from the ground to block the mist. The plants shot up, tangling with the darkness, but the mist pushed back, dissolving the vines like they were nothing more than smoke.

Leo unleashed a torrent of flames, trying to burn away the mist, but it only parted, reforming on the other side.

"This stuff won't stop!" Leo growled, frustration in his voice.

Nora stepped forward, her shadows meeting the mist head-on. The two forces clashed, swirling and twisting around each other in a battle for control. "This isn't just magic," she said, her voice steady. "This is something deeper."

The mist continued to surge toward them, and Finn could feel the pressure building in the air. They couldn't hold it off forever.

"We have to get to the Heart," Finn said urgently. "It's the only way we'll be able to stop this."

The Heart's Call

As they fought their way through the mist, Finn felt a strange pull in his chest—like a silent call, beckoning him forward. It was the Heart, calling out to them, its magic weak but still alive.

"I can feel it," Finn said, his voice filled with urgency. "The Heart is calling us. We're close."

The group pushed forward, moving faster now, their feet pounding against the shifting ground. The mist continued to swirl around them, but they pressed on, determined to reach the Heart before it was too late.

The trees began to thin, and in the distance, they could see the faint glow of the Heart's magic—a soft, pulsing light that flickered like a dying flame. The closer they got, the stronger the pull became, guiding them toward the source of the magic that had been protecting Ravenerode for so long.

But the darkness was moving faster.

Suddenly, the ground in front of them erupted, and from the earth rose a towering figure, its body made of shadow and mist. It was massive, looming over them with eyes that glowed a sickly red. The air around it crackled with dark energy, and the forest seemed to tremble in its presence.

The creature's voice was a low, rumbling growl, filled with malice and ancient power. "You will not reach the Heart."

Finn's breath caught in his throat. The darkness had taken form.

The Battle Begins

Leo didn't hesitate. His flames roared to life, hotter and brighter than ever before, and he launched a fiery attack at the creature. The flames struck the figure, but instead of recoiling, it absorbed the fire, growing larger as the shadows around it thickened.

"Fire makes it stronger!" Leo shouted, stepping back in shock.

"We need to weaken it!" Sophie called out, her mind racing. She raised her hands, summoning more vines from the ground to try to entangle the creature, but the shadow tendrils tore through them effortlessly.

Nora stepped forward, her shadows swirling around her like a protective barrier. "It's feeding off the magic around us. We have to cut it off from the Heart's power."

"But how?" Maya asked, her voice strained as she tried to hold the earth steady beneath them. "The Heart's magic is connected to everything here."

Finn tightened his grip on his staff, his wind magic swirling around him. The creature was too strong for them to take head-on, but they couldn't let it reach the Heart. If they didn't find a way to stop it, everything they had fought for would be lost.

"We need to split up," Finn said suddenly, his mind racing. "Leo, Sophie, and I will hold it off. Maya and Nora, you two get to the Heart. If you can connect with its magic, you might be able to weaken the creature."

Maya hesitated, glancing at the looming figure. "Are you sure?"

"We don't have a choice," Finn said, his voice filled with determination. "The Heart is the only thing that can stop this."

Nora nodded, her shadows already moving. "We'll find a way."

A Desperate Plan

As Maya and Nora broke off toward the Heart, Finn, Leo, and Sophie braced themselves for the coming battle. The creature's shadowy form surged forward, its red eyes locked on them, filled with malice.

"We just need to hold it off," Finn reminded them. "We can't let it get past us."

Leo's flames flickered, but he nodded, focusing his energy. "I'll keep it distracted."

Sophie, her hands trembling slightly, took a deep breath. "We can do this."

The creature let out a deafening roar and charged. Leo struck first, launching a barrage of fireballs at the creature's feet, trying to force it back. The flames didn't hurt it, but they slowed its advance.

Sophie summoned every bit of magic she had, calling on the plants and vines around them to form a thick wall of greenery between them and the creature. It wouldn't hold for long, but it bought them time.

Finn, wind swirling around him, summoned a powerful gust, pushing the creature back. But the creature was relentless, absorbing the magic around it and growing stronger with each attack.

At the Heart

Meanwhile, Maya and Nora sprinted toward the glowing light of the Heart. The magic pulsed weakly, but it was still there, flickering like a dying ember.

"We're almost there," Maya said, her voice filled with urgency. As they reached the Heart, Maya pressed her hands to the ground, trying to connect with the magic beneath them. The earth responded, but it was weak, drained from the darkness that was consuming it.

Nora, her shadows flickering around her, stepped closer to the Heart. "It's trying to protect itself," she said quietly. "But it's not strong enough."

Maya's brow furrowed in concentration. "We need to give it more power. If we can strengthen the Heart, we can weaken the creature."

Nora nodded, her shadows blending with the light of the Heart. "Let's do this."

Together, they began channeling their magic into the Heart, feeding it the energy it needed to push back against the darkness.

Chapter 37

The Battle for the Heart

The darkness loomed large, its massive, shadowy form towering over Finn, Leo, and Sophie as they braced for the next wave of attacks. The creature, seemingly feeding off the very magic of Ravenerode, moved with a slow, deliberate menace. Each step it took sent tremors through the earth, and the shadows around it swirled in chaotic patterns, lashing out like whips of dark energy.

"We need to keep it back!" Finn shouted over the deafening roar of the creature. His wind magic swirled fiercely around him, forming a barrier that slowed the creature's advance. But Finn could feel it—a strain, a weariness creeping in. The creature was stronger than anything they'd faced before, and every strike it absorbed only made it more powerful.

Leo gritted his teeth, flames roaring in his hands as he sent a blast of fire at the creature's legs. The fire hit, but once again, it merely passed through the shadowy figure, dissipating into nothing.

"This thing's like a void!" Leo growled, frustration in his voice. "We need a new plan!"

Sophie, her brow furrowed in concentration, summoned more vines from the earth, trying to entangle the creature's legs. But the vines barely touched its form before shriveling into dust. "It's absorbing everything we throw at it," she muttered. "We need to weaken it somehow!"

Finn could feel the pressure mounting. They were running out of options, and the creature wasn't slowing down. They couldn't hold it off forever—not without the Heart's magic to help them.

At the Heart's Core

Meanwhile, at the center of the forest, Maya and Nora stood before the Heart of Ravenerode—a glowing, pulsating orb of pure magic that flickered weakly with each passing moment. The air around it was thick with tension, and the magic it emitted, once vibrant and strong, now felt fragile, as though it were on the verge of collapse.

Maya pressed her hands to the ground, her connection to the earth deepening as she tried to draw more power from the forest. "The Heart is still fighting," she said, her voice filled with urgency. "But it's weak. The darkness is draining it."

Nora, her shadows swirling around her like protective armor, stepped closer to the Heart. "We need to give it more power," she said, her voice calm but determined. "If we can strengthen the Heart, we can push the darkness back."

Maya nodded, her eyes filled with determination. "Then we do it. We give it everything we have."

Together, they knelt before the Heart, their hands outstretched toward the glowing orb. Maya channeled the energy of the earth, the life force of Ravenerode, into the Heart, while Nora wove her shadows into the magic, fortifying the Heart's defenses. The ground beneath them pulsed in response, and slowly, the Heart's glow grew brighter, stronger.

"It's working," Maya whispered, her voice filled with hope. "The Heart is getting stronger."

But just as the Heart's magic began to swell, a wave of dark energy surged from the forest, crashing against the Heart's core like a tidal wave. The force of it sent Maya and Nora reeling back, and the Heart flickered once more, its light dimming.

Nora's breath caught in her throat. "The creature—it's drawing the magic away from the Heart. If we don't stop it, the Heart will collapse."

A Desperate Move

Back at the front line, Finn, Leo, and Sophie struggled to hold the creature at bay. The dark figure, now larger and more imposing, moved closer with each passing second, its shadowy tendrils lashing out, pushing through their defenses.

"We can't keep this up!" Leo shouted, his flames flickering weakly in his hands. "It's too strong!"

Finn knew he was right. The creature was feeding off the Heart's magic, growing more powerful with every moment. If they didn't act soon, it would reach the Heart—and then all of Ravenerode would be lost.

"We need to stop it from drawing power!" Finn called out, his mind racing for a solution.

Sophie's eyes widened as an idea formed in her mind. "The creature is connected to the Heart!" she said, her voice filled with realization. "If we cut off its connection to the magic, we can weaken it!"

"How?" Leo asked, his frustration mounting.

Sophie glanced at the ground, her mind working quickly. "We disrupt the flow of magic. The creature is drawing power from the Heart through the earth. If we break the connection, we can stop it from getting stronger."

Finn's heart pounded in his chest. It was a long shot, but it was their only option. "Do it, Sophie," he said, his voice filled with determination.

Sophie knelt down, pressing her hands to the earth. She could feel the magic flowing beneath the surface, connecting the creature to the Heart. With a deep breath, she summoned all of her strength and commanded the vines and roots to shift, to move, to break the connection between the creature and the magic.

The ground trembled beneath them as the roots twisted and snapped, breaking the flow of magic. The creature let out a deafening roar, its form flickering as it stumbled back, weakened by the disruption.

"It's working!" Finn shouted, his wind magic swirling around him as he pressed the advantage. "We've weakened it!"

Leo grinned, flames blazing brighter in his hands. "Let's finish this!"

The Final Push

With the creature momentarily weakened, Finn, Leo, and Sophie launched their final attack. Finn summoned a powerful gust of wind, pushing the creature back, while Leo unleashed a torrent of flames that swirled around the shadowy figure, burning away the darkness. Sophie, her connection to the earth stronger than ever, commanded the vines to rise once more, entangling the creature's legs and holding it in place.

The creature roared in fury, its shadowy form flickering and wavering. It tried to lash out, but the combined force of their magic was too strong. Slowly, the darkness began to unravel, dissolving into the air like smoke.

At the same time, Maya and Nora, their energy fully focused on the Heart, poured every ounce of their magic into the glowing orb. The Heart pulsed brighter and brighter, its light growing stronger with each passing moment.

And then, with a final, blinding flash of light, the creature let out one last, agonized roar and dissolved completely, leaving nothing but silence in its wake.

The Heart Restored

As the darkness faded, the forest grew still. The oppressive weight that had hung in the air lifted, and the magic of Ravenerode pulsed once more, stronger and more vibrant than before. The Heart, now fully restored, glowed brightly in the center of the forest, its light filling the clearing with warmth and life.

Maya and Nora, exhausted but relieved, stood before the Heart, their hands still outstretched. "We did it," Maya whispered, her voice filled with awe. "The Heart is safe."

Nora nodded, her shadows flickering gently around her. "For now."

Finn, Leo, and Sophie approached, their breaths ragged but triumphant. The battle was over, but the weight of what they had just faced still lingered in the air.

"We stopped it," Finn said, his voice steady but filled with exhaustion. "But this isn't over."

Sophie glanced at the glowing Heart, her mind still racing. "The darkness came for the Heart once. It might come again."

Leo, his flames now extinguished, crossed his arms and let out a long breath. "Let it. We'll be ready."

A New Beginning

The five friends stood together, the glow of the Heart illuminating the forest around them. They had faced the darkness and emerged victorious, but they knew their journey was far from over. The magic of Ravenerode was powerful, but so were the forces that sought to destroy it.

"We're the protectors of this place now," Finn said, his voice filled with resolve. "The Heart chose us for a reason. And we're not going to let anything happen to it."

Maya smiled faintly, her connection to the earth stronger than ever. "We'll stand by the Heart, no matter what."

Nora's shadows swirled around her, her gaze sharp and determined. "The darkness isn't gone. But neither are we."

Sophie, her hand resting on the ground, felt the pulse of the Heart beneath her fingers. "This is just the beginning."

With the Heart restored and the darkness pushed back, the friends knew they had found their true purpose: to protect the magic of Ravenerode and ensure that the Heart's light would never fade.

Together, they turned toward the future, knowing that no matter what challenges lay ahead, they would face them united—guardians of the Heart, protectors of Ravenerode.

As the Heart of Ravenerode pulsed with renewed life, the forest settled into a peaceful silence. The five friends stood together, watching the light fade into the trees, feeling the weight of their new roles as protectors.

But deep in the shadows of the forest, where the light of the Heart could not reach, something stirred. The air grew cold, and a faint whisper echoed through the trees—too soft for anyone to hear, but strong enough to send a ripple through the ancient magic of Ravenerode.

The darkness had been pushed back, but it was not gone. And soon, it would rise again.

To be continued...

www.ingramcontent.com/pod-product-compliance
Lightning Source LLC
Chambersburg PA
CBHW062149150726
47991CB00006B/2216